To Jennifer,
Emily and Isabelle.
With love.

DOCTOR WHO
THE HIGHLANDERS

Based on the BBC television serial by Gerry Davis and Elwyn Jones by arrangement with the British Broadcasting Corporation

Gerry Davis

Number 90
in the
Doctor Who Library

A TARGET BOOK

published by
the Paperback Division of
W. H. ALLEN & Co. PLC

A Target Book
Published in 1984
By the Paperback Division of
W. H. Allen & Co. PLC
44 Hill Street, London W1X 8LB

First published in Great Britain by
W. H. Allen & Co. PLC 1984

The BBC producer of *The Highlanders* was Innes Lloyd,
the director was Hugh David.

Printed and bound in Great Britain by
Anchor Brendon Ltd, Tiptree, Essex

ISBN 0 426 19676 7

CONTENTS

1

Where are We?

The TARDIS was slowly materialising in the middle of a clump of brambles and ferns. Finally, the burning motors died down, the door opened, and out jumped Ben, followed by Polly. Then the Doctor emerged, wearing his shabby old frock coat and rather baggy check trousers. Ben looked around eagerly. They were in the middle of a small overgrown hollow. The ground was grassy and very damp. Ben used his arm to push aside some brambles to give the others room to get clear of the TARDIS.

'Here, Polly,' said Ben. 'Look at this. What's it look like to you?'

Polly, who was following Ben, stopped, shivered, and tried to prize away an intrusive strand of brambles which had caught her arm. She was clad in her mini-skirt and T-shirt, and it was undeniably chilly, especially after the warmth of the TARDIS's interior. 'It's certainly cold and damp,' Polly said. 'I don't think I like this place very much.'

Behind them, the Doctor looked around drawing his own conclusions, but as usual said nothing. He liked to have his young companions make their own minds up about the various strange locations the TARDIS arrived in.

' 'Ere, what's it remind you of?' said Ben, excitedly. 'Cold . . . damp. Where'd you think we are, Princess?'

Polly moved backwards and caught her thigh on

7

another prickly clump of brambles. She yelled crossly: 'How do I know? And don't call me "Princess." '

'Don't you see, Princess?' said Ben. 'It's England. Where else could it be? What other country is as wet as this? What do you think, Doctor?'

The Doctor was listening intently. He motioned them to keep quiet and listen.

Ben and Polly became aware of a distant murmur over which could be heard the sounds of musket-fire, cries and shouts, and the boom of cannons firing.

'Cor,' said Ben. 'That proves it! It's a soccer match. We've come on Cup Final night! It sounds like the Spurs' Supporters' Club.'

'Shush, Ben,' said Polly, as the noise of battle increased. There was a loud cannon boom which seemed to come from just over the next hill. They heard a piercing whistle, then, crashing through the trees at the end of the hollow and rolling almost to their feet, a black iron cannon-ball appeared. It landed only a foot away from the Doctor. He immediately turned and started back for the TARDIS. 'That's it!' he said, 'come back inside.'

Polly turned, disappointed. 'But if this is England?'

The Doctor turned. 'Either way I don't like it,' he said. 'There's a battle in progress – not so very far away from here.'

Ben, meanwhile, was on his knees examining the cannon-ball. 'Hey,' he said, 'nothing to be alarmed about. It's an old time cannon-ball. It's probably one of them, y'know, historical societies playing soldier.' He touched it gingerly and pulled his hand away, sucking his finger. 'Ain't half hot!'

The Doctor turned and looked at the cannon-ball. 'A ten-pounder. A little careless for an historical society to play around with it, don't you think?'

Polly, meanwhile, was taking in the grass, the brambles, and the wild flowers. 'Listen,' she said. 'I'm

8

sure we're back in England somewhere. Look,' she pointed. 'Dogroses. They only seem to grow in the British Isles. Can't we stay for a little while, Doctor, and find out what's happening here?'

'Well, I'm going to take a shufty over this hill,' said Ben.

'I'd advise you not to,' rejoined the Doctor.

Polly turned to him. 'Doctor,' she said, 'anyone would think you're afraid.'

'Yes, they would, wouldn't they? And that's exactly what I am. If you had any sense you'd be afraid, too. These things,' the Doctor kicked the cannon-ball, 'may be old-fashioned but they can do a lot of damage.'

Polly looked after Ben, who was now scrambling up the small rise at the end of the hollow. 'Come on, we can't let Ben go up alone, can we?'

'You two get me into more trouble . . .' began the Doctor, but Polly had already set off running up the hill after Ben, her long legs flashing through the undergrowth. The Doctor shrugged, took one more look at the cannon-ball and followed them.

If they had been able to see over the hill they might have been more inclined to follow the Doctor's advice. In the next valley a small group of Highlanders were fleeing from the Redcoats.

A few hours previously, the largely Highland Scottish troops of Prince Charles Edward, better known as Bonnie Prince Charlie, had drawn up their battle lines against the English and German Army led by the Duke of Cumberland, who were fighting for King George. What was at stake was the entire future of the British monarchy.

The English had been alienated by the autocratic Scottish Stuart Kings, and some forty years before had thrown them out of the United Kingdom, replacing them with the Hanoverian German Georges. Now

9

Prince Charles Edward, also known as the Young Pretender and the latest in the line of Stuart claimants to the throne of England, had come to Scotland and raised his standard. He gathered together a large army among the Scottish Highland clans and marched south to take England.

The Highland army marched as far south as Derby, and indeed might well have taken over the country had they not lost their nerve at the last moment and retreated to what they considered was the safety of the Scottish glens.

But the delay was to cost them dear. King George and his supporters soon rounded up an army of English and German regiments, and even a number of Scottish troops loyal to King George who did not like the prospect of another erratic Stuart king on the throne.

The result was the battle known as Culloden Moor. It was an unequal contest right from the start. Despite the lion-like courage of the Scots, the iron discipline of the Redcoats and their deadly firepower wiped out row after row of the charging, kilted Highland clansmen.

Eventually, flesh and blood could stand no more of the withering musket and cannon-fire from the British and German lines. The Highlanders broke ranks and started to flee the battlefield.

The Duke of Cumberland gave the order to pursue the Scots and give no quarter. The British troops, angered at the attempted takeover of their country by the Scots, needed little inducement and chased the fleeing Highlanders throughout the Scottish Glens.

Among the fleeing Scots was a small group from the clan McLaren and their followers. Colin McLaren, the leader of the clan, was badly wounded, and was being supported by his son Alexander and the bagpiper of the McLarens, young Jamie McCrimmon. Beside them as they struggled through the heather, half dragging the tall, white-haired clan chieftain, was Alexander's sister

Kirsty. Normally a pretty, red-headed Highland lassie, Kirsty was bedraggled, her face smudged with dirt, her beautiful red hair a tangled mess. She had followed her father and brother in order to see the expected victory of the Scottish Army. Instead, she had just arrived in time to witness a disaster. Now all four were fleeing desperately from the red-coated soldiers.

They hurried up a winding, rocky path, and turned a corner to confront two Redcoats, each with musket and bayonet at the ready.

Kirsty flung her arms around her father's neck and pulled him to one side, as Alexander drew his long claymore and leaped forward to do battle with them.

The first Redcoat lunged forward, his long steel bayonet stabbing towards the centre of the Highlander's chest. Alexander was too fast for him. He jumped aside and with one glittering sweep, his great broadsword swept upwards. The soldier, slashed from thigh to rib-cage, slowly collapsed back onto the heather as his companion aimed his musket at the Scot. There was a puff of smoke and a loud report. The musket ball missed Alexander's red hair by about an inch, and the Highlander raised the claymore again and sprang forward, yelling the McLaren war-cry.

The frightened soldier dropped his musket and with one startled glance ran back along the path.

When Alexander started after him, the piper, Jamie, called to him to stop. Alexander paused while the soldier scurried away over the hill. He turned back angrily. 'Why did ye do that?' he said.

Jamie turned. 'You're needed here with your father.'

'But yon soldier will be bringing back reinforcements,' said Alexander.

'Then we'd better get out of here quickly,' said Jamie.

Alexander turned, looked down at the dead Redcoat at their feet, and nodded. He turned back to his father and helped him back on his feet.

Meanwhile, the Doctor and his companions were still trying to locate the battle. It was very frustrating. Over the hill the fog had really closed in around them. They could hear the sounds of the battle and, occasionally, there was a flash in the grey distance. But they could see nothing clearly because of the heavy mist.

'Do you know where we are yet, Doctor?' asked Polly. The Doctor looked at her and shook his head.

'No, and if we go much further we won't be able to find our way back to the TARDIS.'

'Hey,' Ben interrupted. 'Look at this.' He was standing on a large rock at the side of the path they were following. There, set against a dry stone wall, was a small cannon.

'What do you make of it?' he asked. The Doctor came up.

'That cannon-ball must have come down 'ere,' Ben continued. He looked down. 'There, look.' He picked up another similar black heavy cannon-ball. 'Exactly like the geezer that just missed us!'

The Doctor glanced closely at the cannon and sniffed it. 'I don't think so,' he said.

'But it is. Look, same size,' said Ben, holding up the cannon-ball. 'This gun hasn't fired for the last hour at least,' the Doctor said.

'Why do you say that?' said Polly.

'It's been spiked,' replied the Doctor.

Ben stared at him. 'Spiked?'

The Doctor pointed to the cannon mouth. 'It's had a spike hammered down inside to stop it being used.'

Ben looked inside the barrel. 'Yeah, Doctor,' he said, 'you're right. It's been spiked.'

Meanwhile, the Doctor was busy examining the inscription cast into the side of the solid iron of the gun. 'Here, Polly, you should be able to work this out.'

Polly glanced at it and read '*Honi soit, qui mal y pense.*' 'Evil to him that evil thinks,' she translated.

12

'We all know what that means, Duchess,' said Ben crossly. He always felt that Polly was a bit, as he put it, 'uppity and toffee-nosed,' and resented her parading her superior knowledge before him. 'It's the motto of the Prince of Wales, right, Doctor?'

'We must have gone back in time,' said Polly, disappointed. 'But when?'

'Well,' said the Doctor, 'I have a theory . . .' He stopped. The others looked at him. 'But I'll tell you later. Meanwhile, isn't that a cottage over there?' He pointed forward to where the mist had cleared slightly. Ahead of them was a small crofter's cottage sunk into the hillside, with a thatched roof, thick stone walls, one small window, and a solid-looking oak door. 'Let's see if we can find someone in there,' said the Doctor.

Ben and Polly started running down the path towards it.

2

The Cottage

Polly was the first one to reach the door. She put her hand on the latch.

'Hold on, Duchess,' said Ben behind her. 'Don't forget there's some sort of argy-bargy going on around here. Let's be a bit careful about what we do, eh?'

'Oh, you mean let you go in first because you're a man,' said Polly sarcastically. Just as Ben resented what he called her 'toffee-nosed' attitude, she resented his 'big brother' protectiveness, especially as she was about a head taller than he was. She swung the doorknob and pulled, but nothing happened.

'Here, let me,' said Ben.

The Doctor had now come up and joined them. Ben put his shoulder to the door, which slowly swung open. He stepped inside, followed by the others.

Inside, the cottage was cramped and plainly furnished. There was a large, blackened fireplace with an iron grill and a pot suspended over a peat fire; a plain, roughcut wooden table, two chairs and a couple of three-legged stools. The floor was covered with coarse rush matting.

Ben stepped forward and began investigating the contents of the pot. 'Stew,' he said. 'Smells good too!'

'Ah!' The Doctor stepped forward, picking up a hat left lying on the table. It was a tam-o'-shanter, a Tartan beret with a silver badge holding a long brown feather. The Doctor was very fond of hats. It was a standing joke in the TARDIS that he could never resist trying on any new hat he came across. This one was no exception. The Doctor pulled on the tam-o'-shanter and turned to the others. 'How do I look?' he said.

Polly giggled. 'Very silly.' Then she glanced more closely at the hat. 'Oh, look. It's got a white band with words on it.'

'What kind of words?' asked the Doctor.

Polly slowly read the antique scrawl: *'With Charles, our brave and merciful Prince Royal, we will die or nobly save our country.'*

'What?' said the Doctor. He pulled off the hat, looked at it with disgust, and slung it back on the table. 'Romantic piffle!'

The Doctor and his companions had been too pre-occupied to notice the door leading to the rear part of the cottage stealthily open behind them. Suddenly, Jamie sprung out and placed a dirk at Ben's chest. Alexander followed and laid his claymore blade across the Doctor's throat. 'You'll pick that up,' he snarled, 'and treat it wi' due respect.'

The Doctor smiled and nodded. 'Of course, of course,' he murmured, and gingerly bent down. 'If you'd just move that sword a little.' Alexander moved the sword away slightly and the Doctor picked up the hat.

'Now give it to me,' said Alexander. The Doctor handed it to him. 'Thank ye. Now this way with ye. Quick.'

Alexander ushered Ben and the Doctor at swordpoint into the back bedroom, and turned to Jamie. 'Take a look outside, Jamie lad – there may be more of them.'

Jamie ran to the door and glanced around. The mist was closing in again, and the sounds of battle had died down. There was no sign of other pursuers. Reassured, he turned back, closed the door, and followed the others through into the bedroom. Inside, there was just a small rough wooden cot with bracken for a mattress on which the wounded Laird McLaren was lying. The only other

15

furnishing was a roughly carved spinning-wheel. As the Doctor and his companions entered with Alexander's claymore behind them, prodding them, Colin tried to rise.

'We must away! We must away to the cave,' he cried.

But Kirsty pushed him down. 'You're no in a fit state to travel, father.'

'We have the supplies in the cave,' said Colin. 'And arms. We need must get there. We'll aye be safe in the cave.' He stopped as his eyes began to focus on the Doctor and his companions. 'Who are these folk?'

Alexander shrugged his shoulders. 'I ken not. They are no honest Scots, that's for certain. They threw down the Prince's cockade.'

'Cockade?' said Polly.

'What Prince?' said Ben.

The Doctor smiled and nodded a confirmation of something he'd obviously been pondering. 'Prince Charles Edward, of course. Bonnie Prince Charlie.'

'There!' said Alexander. 'Ya heard that accent, did ye? I thought so. English, the three of them. Camp followers of the Duke of Cumberland. Come to steal from the dead. Shall I kill them now?' He raised his claymore. Polly retreated behind Ben. The Doctor and Ben stood their ground. Then Colin shook his head. 'Wait,' he said to Alexander. 'Perhaps they'd like to say a wee prayer before they die.'

'Die?' echoed the Doctor.

'Die for what?' demanded Polly. 'You can't mean to kill us all in cold blood.'

'Yeah! We've done nothing, mate,' Ben added.

Alexander frowned. 'Our blood's warm enough, dinna fear. Your English troopers give no quarter to men, women or bairns.'

Polly shrunk back, frightened. 'Doctor, tell them who we are.'

Kirsty turned. '*Doctor,*' she said. She went over and

16

seized Alexander's arm. 'Did you hear what she said? She called him *Doctor.*'

Alexander pushed Kirsty back. 'Get back to your father,' he said.

'Hold awhile,' insisted Kirsty. 'We have sore need of a doctor.'

Colin shook his head, closing his eyes in pain. 'Nay,' he said. 'Nay, doctor.' His head shook slightly, and then he slumped back unconscious.

'Father.' Kirsty leapt forward and felt for his heartbeat.

'How is he?' asked Alexander.

'He's still alive – but he needs help.'

Alexander stood uncertainly for a minute, with the bloodstained sword held threateningly before the Doctor and Ben, then Kirsty stepped forward and stood between the Doctor and Alexander. 'You can kill him afterwards, but let him help the Laird first.'

Alexander turned around uncertainly, looking at the door, which gave Ben an opportunity. He had noticed a pistol down at the side of the unconscious Laird. Now he leapt forward, grabbed it and pointed it at Alexander and Jamie, pulling the hammer back and cocking it.

Kirsty shrieked, backing away; behind her, Jamie and Alexander started forward.

Ben turned the pistol and held the muzzle against Colin's temple. 'Back. Both of you, or your Laird won't need no more doctors.'

The two men faltered irresolutely.

'Do what he says,' said Kirsty. 'Please.'

'I really think you'd better give me that thing,' said the Doctor. He stepped forward and held his hand out for Alexander's sword. For a moment it seemed as though Alexander was going to lunge forward; then the Highlander dropped his sword.

'And the other one,' Ben called. A moment's hesitation, and Jamie flung down his dirk beside the claymore.

'That's much better,' said the Doctor. He bent down and picked up the weapons. He handed the dagger to Polly and put the claymore under the cot. 'Now, if you'd just step back and give us a little more room . . .'

After a moment's hesitation, Alexander and Jamie stepped back.

'That's better. Now,' said the Doctor, 'we can look at the patient.' He turned to Kirsty. 'I think we need some fresh water for this wound.'

Kirsty stood irresolute, staring as though she did not comprehend him. The Doctor unhooked a leather bucket from a rough wooden peg on the wall and handed it to her. 'Here we are. You'll find a spring just a short way back up the track.'

'I'll not leave my father,' said Kirsty.

'Don't worry,' said the Doctor. 'We won't harm him. You do want me to help him, don't you?'

Kirsty remained by her father, staring suspiciously. The Doctor shrugged and turned to Polly. 'Will you go with her, Polly?'

'Of course, Doctor.'

'Off with you both, then.'

Polly turned to Kirsty. She picked up the bucket. 'Your father will be perfectly safe with the Doctor. Come on.'

Alexander had now relaxed a little. He nodded towards Colin. 'Go,' he said. 'And take Father's spy-glass with ye. Watch out for the Sassenach dragoons.'

Still glancing suspiciously at the Doctor, Kirsty went over, took a small brass telescope from her father's belt, and joined Polly by the door. The girls went out together.

Meanwhile, the Doctor had unbuttoned Colin's bloodstained coat and was examining his shoulder. It was a deep wound. 'Musket-ball?' the Doctor looked enquiringly over at Alexander.

Alexander nodded. 'Aye.'

18

'It looks clean enough,' said the Doctor, 'but we'll have to bandage it. I wonder if I have any antiseptic on me. I usually carry a little iodine – one never knows when it will come in handy.'

'Anti what?' asked Alexander, frowning.

'Some medicine – er – herbs . . . to heal the wound,' explained the Doctor.

Alexander started forward menacingly. 'Ye'll no poison my father!'

The Doctor had now found a small bottle of iodine in his pocket. He held it up. 'It's certainly not poison,' he said as he opened it and put a small dab on his tongue.

'There. See?' He grimaced. 'It doesn't taste very nice, but it's certainly not harmful.'

Reassured, Alexander nodded. The Doctor turned back to the wounded Laird. 'I think you can put that thing away now,' he said to Ben.

Ben looked over at the others and shook his head.

'Oh, they'll be all right,' said the Doctor. 'They can see we mean them no harm.' He turned around. 'Will you both give me your word you will not attack us? We're only trying to save your Laird from bleeding to death.'

Alexander nodded solemnly. The Doctor looked at Jamie, who also nodded. 'You have our word.'

'All right, Ben, you can put the gun down now,' said the Doctor.

'What? You're not going to trust these blokes?'

'A Highlander's word,' said the Doctor, 'is his bond.' The pistol wavered uncertainly in Ben's hand.

'At least keep it out of my way,' added the Doctor.

Ben shrugged. He never understood what the Doctor was up to. He tossed the gun onto the table and it went off with a deafening bang, shattering one of the earthenware jugs on the shelf by the bed.

'Ya fool,' said Alexander.

'You'll bring every English soldier within miles around here,' said Jamie.

'Well,' asked Ben, 'what's so wrong with that? If they're English, we got nothing to worry about, have we?'

The Doctor looked up. 'Oh dear. You should have spent more time with your history books, Ben.'

'Eh?' said Ben uncomprehendingly.

Jamie looked through the small window. 'Whist ye!'

Alexander ran to the door and looked out. 'Redcoats,' he turned back inside. 'There's six or more of them. They'll slaughter us like rats in a trap here.' He ran over and fished out the claymore from under the bed.

The Doctor stepped forward and stopped him with a hand on his shoulder, and for a moment Alexander seemed about to forget his promise and run him through.

'You won't stand a chance with that,' said the Doctor. 'We must use our wits in this situation.' Alexander shook his head fiercely. 'You'll just have to trust me, won't you?' said the Doctor. He turned and started pouring the iodine over the Laird's wound. The Laird stirred in pain.

Jamie was looking out of the tiny window. 'They seem to be moving off,' he said. 'Perhaps they won't come inside.'

3

The Captives

Algernon Ffinch was the very picture of a British officer from the mid 18th century. Elegantly turned out from his tricorn hat to his white stockings and buckled shoes, Algernon was handsome and had that ramrod stiffness in his spine that British officers throughout the centuries have always favoured.

He was standing on top of a small hill, gazing down the glen towards the cottage in which the Doctor and the Highland refugees were taking cover. Beside him there was a sergeant who presented a total contrast to the elegant, foppish Algernon. Sergeant Klegg was short, very broadly built, and after twenty years in the British army had seen every sort of action and felt himself a match for any situation. The Sergeant saluted and pointed down towards the cottage.

'We've sighted some rebels, sir. There was a shot, seemed to come from that cottage.'

'Rebels? Well, it's about time. They all seem to have melted into the heather.'

'Them cavalry blokes, the dragoons, were ahead of us.'

'Well,' Algernon shrugged his shoulders, 'I suppose they've driven them all the way to Glasgow by now. I wish they'd left us some pickings, though.'

'Those wot got away took their possessions with them, sir.'

Algernon nodded wearily. 'Let's hope so. Take two

men round to the rear of the cottage, Sergeant, we'll outflank them.'

'Yes sir.' The Sergeant turned and signalled to two of his men. 'Hey, you two! Cut down there quick. And don't make too much noise about it!'

Algernon turned. 'Tell them to shoot first, and take no risks. Remember, these rebels will be desperate men by now. Savages, the lot of them.'

'Sir.' The Sergeant saluted and followed in the path of the two men.

Algernon turned to the remainder of his platoon, some fourteen soldiers. 'Right, men,' he called. 'Fix bayonets and advance in battle order.'

The soldiers with their red coats crossed with pipeclayed bandoliers, drew their bayonets out of their scabbards and fixed them to the ends of their long muskets. They spread out and started moving down the side of the glen through the thick heather towards the cottage.

Inside the cottage, the atmosphere was tense. Alexander, disregarding the Doctor and Ben's pistol, reached for his sword and went to the door. Jamie turned and ran after him.

'Must we be caught here like rats in a trap? We must run for it, mon.'

Alexander spoke through clenched teeth. 'And leave the Laird to their mercy? There is one chance and it's aye a slender one. I will try and draw them away from this cottage.'

The Doctor looked up from the Laird; he had finished bandaging the man's wound. 'Wait a minute . . .'

But Alexander was already out of the cottage and running out to face the oncoming English troops. He raised his claymore sword high above his head and called the bloodcurdling shrill rallying cry of Clan McLaren.

'Creag an tuire.'

There was a ragged chorus of musketry as the soldiers fell on one knee, raised their muskets, and fired at the Highlander. One of the musket-balls hit Alexander in the shoulder, and he staggered but continued his advance up towards the oncoming English troopers. The second rank of the English Redcoats fired. Alexander jerked convulsively as the balls hit him and slowly crumpled forward. He raised his claymore for one last act of defiance, but the sword dropped from his hand and he fell over face downward in the heather.

Jamie, standing by the door of the cottage, had witnessed it all and, upset, shrank back covering his eyes with his hand, unable to stand the sight of his friend's gallant but futile death. Behind him, Ben and the Doctor watched transfixed, as the Sergeant and the two troopers took up positions behind them with levelled bayonets.

'Surrender in the King's name!' The Sergant's rough voice startled the three. Jamie looked wildly around for escape but, caught between the two troopers and the advancing circle of Redcoats, realised that escape was out of the question. Ben looked curiously at the Sergeant's red uniform and the tall hat.

'Blimey,' he said, 'it's nice to hear a London voice again.'

The Sergeant stepped forward fearfully. 'Silence you rebel dog.'

Ben started back. 'Rebel, what you talking about? I'm no rebel. Me and the Doctor here, we just arrived.'

The Sergeant shrugged his shoulders. 'Deserter, then. You'll hang just the same.'

'Hang!' said Ben, astonished. 'Me? I'm on your side, you can't –' But the Doctor put his hand on Ben's shoulder and stepped forward.

To Ben's astonishment, the Doctor spoke in a heavy German accent. 'I am glad you hav come, Sergeant,' he said. 'I hav been vaiting for an escort.' The Sergeant was astonished at the Doctor's easy authority and his strange clothes.

'Who do you think you are then?' he said.

'Ven you find out,' said the Doctor, 'you vill perhaps learn to keep a civil tongue in your head, nein? Are you in charge here?'

While the Sergeant stared at him, speechless at being spoken to in this way by a man he considered one of the rebels, Algernon Ffinch came up to them having overheard the Doctor's words. 'No,' he said, 'I'm the officer here.'

The Doctor turned to him and bowed. 'Ah, a gentleman at last. Doctor von Verner at your service.' He clicked his heels and bowed again.

'Oh,' said Algernon. 'One of those demned froggies that came over with the Pretender, eh?'

That was too much for Ben. 'Froggies!' he said. 'Do we look like froggies?' He turned to the Doctor. 'He thinks we're French.'

The Doctor shook his head. 'Ach, no. I am German, from Hanover where your King George comes from. And I speak English much better than he does.'

The Sergeant who had been keeping his temper with some difficulty now burst out. ' 'Ear that, sir? Treason it is! Shall I hang them now?'

Algernon shook his head. 'No,' he said. 'W – wait a moment.' He stumbled slightly over his consonants in a way approved by the London dandies of the time. He stepped into the cottage and looked around. 'Let's see who else we have here.'

Jamie tried to get between the officer and the bedroom where the Laird was resting, but the troopers seized hold of him and pulled him out of the way. Algernon walked through, followed by Ben, the Doctor, and the Sergeant, and looked over at the now unconscious Colin lying on the bracken bed.

'Who is that man?' he said. He turned to Jamie.

'Colin McLaren, the Laird,' said Jamie. 'And I'm his piper, Jamie McCrimmon, ye ken.'

The Sergeant turned and spat on the floor. 'A poor lot, sir,' he said. 'We'll get no decent pickings here. Let's hang them and have done.'

Ben turned on him. 'You're a right shower, you are. What have we done? – Nothing. And what have you got against them two? They lost a battle, right? Doesn't that make them prisoners of war?'

Algernon turned slightly towards Ben and spoke over his shoulder coldly. 'Rebels are not treated as p-p-p-prisoners of war,' he said. He turned to the Sergeant as he drew out a lace handkerchief from his sleeve, holding it to his nose against the close smell of the cottage. 'Right, Sergeant, you may prepare to hang them.'

The Sergeant saluted. 'Sir.' He turned to the men. 'You, you, take 'em through there and hang them.'

Ben could hardly speak, he was so astonished. The Doctor stood back, considering, as two of the troopers pulled Colin to his feet, still half conscious, and dragged him out of the door. Jamie tried to run up to them but the other two men held him fast.

'Ya canna do that,' he said. 'He's . . .'

'And take him too,' said the Sergeant. 'He's next.'

The Doctor stepped forward. 'I vould advise you not to do this,' he said. He turned. 'Ben here and myself, ve are witnesses, no?'

Algernon turned to consider him for a moment. 'Yes,' he said, 'that's right,' He called after the Sergeant. 'And when you're done with those two, you can hang these riffraff.' He turned and walked out of the room.

Solicitor Grey was sitting on the high seat of a supply wagon for the Duke of Cumberland's British Army. He had been watching the battle through a telescope, which he now shut up and placed back in a leather case beside him on the seat. He was a tall, thin man with a face the colour of his name. In fact, everything about the solicitor was grey, from his mud-spattered coat to his long, lank grey hair carefully held back in a bow in the manner of the period, and his long grey riding boots. His voice had the dusty echo of the law chambers and the penetrating edge acquired from years of pleading cases in court. There was a dangerous stillness about the man. He never allowed his feelings to get in the way of his business, and everything was considered in a purely logical light without the softening shadow of ordinary humanity or human feelings.

He turned to look down at his clerk, Perkins, who was standing by an upturned barrel on which he was spreading out a cold lunch for his master. Perkins was a complete contrast to his master. His clothes were mussed up and untidy compared with the solicitor's neatly tied cravat and well-buttoned waistcoat. Perkins, a short, slightly fat man, looked as though his buttons were in the wrong holes. His pockets bulged, his sleeves were ragged at the ends, and his hands were covered with inkstains because Perkins was a solicitor's clerk, and his main duties were the endless copying and drafting of legal documents.

Grey started clambering down from the wagon. 'Not a very inspiring battle, wouldn't you say, Perkins?'

Perkins looked up. 'Don't really know, sir. I've never seen a battle before.' He spoke with a slight Cockney accent, in contrast to Grey's neutral, even tones.

Grey shrugged his shoulders. 'This one was over in but a brief hour. I have never seen brave fellows so poorly led.' He brought out a handkerchief and wiped dust from the wagon off his hands. 'Now,' he continued, 'our brave Duke's troops are busy bayoneting the wounded. Such a waste of manpower.' He shook his head in disgust and handed the telescope to Perkins, who carefully put it away in the large food hamper beside the barrel. 'Well,' said Grey, yawning and stretching, 'at least it's given me an appetite. I think I'll have a little wine.'

Perkins rubbed his hands enthusiastically, his eyes lighting up at the mention of food. 'Oh, yes sir, yes sir.' He indicated the barrel top on which he had laid out cold chicken, ham, bread, and a bottle of red wine. He started to pour a glass of wine for his master. 'I'm quite ready for it, sir,' he said. 'It must be this sharp northern air, sir. Gives one quite an appetite, doesn't it?'

As he talked, two soldiers came along, half dragging the wounded Highlander and urging him on with kicks and blows. As he passed, the Scot turned and looked longingly at the food.

'You'll get plenty to eat where you're going, old mate, never fear,' said one of the soldiers, laughing at the man.

'Yeah,' said the other soldier, 'worms, most like. Get on with you.' And he kicked the Highlander again as they walked away up the path.

Grey sat down on an upturned crate set beside the barrel and held the wine up to examine it for pieces of floating cork. 'All these fine fellows,' he said, 'sturdy, used to hard work and little food. Think what a price such men would fetch in Barbados, or Jamaica, Perkins.'

Perkins, who had been trying to stuff a piece of chicken in his mouth while his master was distracted looking at the wounded Highlander, swallowed it hastily. 'A pretty penny, no doubt sir. No doubt at all.'

'Indeed,' continued Grey. 'And I'll have them, Perkins. I did not leave a thriving legal practice at Lincoln's Inn just for the honour of serving King George as his Commissioner of Prisons.' He picked up a napkin Perkins had neatly folded and placed on the barrel, and fastidiously tied it around his neck. Perkins had filled a plate for his master with meat, cheese, onions and bread, and handed it to Grey.

'I thought there was more behind it, sir.'

'With Mr Trask and his ship at our service, we may expect to clear some measure of profit from this rebellion, eh Mr Perkins?'

'Oh yes, sir.'

'Depending, of course, on how many of these wretched rebels we can deliver from His Majesty's over-zealous soldiers.' Grey took a mouthful of the red wine and then, suddenly rising as he tasted it, spat it into Perkins' face. Perkins started back in surprise, gaping at his master as he brought out a handkerchief and started wiping his face. Grey dabbed at his mouth with a fine lace handkerchief he carried in his top pocket and as though nothing untoward had occurred, said, 'I thought so, Perkins. The wine was corked. If you wish to continue in my service you'll have to be more careful, won't you, Perkins?' He turned and glanced at the frightened little man beside him, and for a moment the sinister force of the lawyer became apparent as Perkins shrank back. 'You'll have to be *much* more careful, won't you, Perkins?' Grey repeated.

Perkins nodded apologetically, stumbling over his words. 'I'm very sorry, sir. My apologies. It really won't happen again, I promise you, sir.' As he spoke there was a ragged burst of musketry. Grey mounted the step of the wagon and looked over in the distance.

The mist was beginning to clear and around them they could now make out the dimensions of the battlefield of Culloden Moor, with small groups of Redcoats scouring the brakes and pitches for the few knots of Highlanders still left.

Grey frowned. 'We must be about our duties, although we've nothing but corpses left on the battlefield.' He looked down at Perkins and smiled a cold smile. 'And corpses are little use to us, eh Perkins? Come,' he said, 'let's go.' Without more ado, Grey jumped from the wagon and strode off, leaving the small, fat clerk hastily shoving the food back into the hamper.

Perkins picked up the wine and held it up to the light, but couldn't see what his master was annoyed about. He shrugged and, raising the bottle to his mouth, took a deep swig.

'Perkins!' Grey's urgent tone came back to him. The solicitor was striding away across the moor. Perkins, almost choking, flung the bottle away in the heather then, grabbing the hamper, scrambled after his master.

4

The Handsome Lieutenant

Following the Scots girl's intense gaze, Polly looked down towards the cottage to see the Redcoats and the soldiers clustered around an oak tree which stood just outside the front door.

'What are they doing?' asked Polly.

Kirsty brought the Laird's telescope out of her pocket and steadied it against her arm. Through the eyepiece she could clearly make out her father and Jamie, and the rope with the noose hung over a branch of the tree. She turned to Polly and pulled her arm, dragging her down into the heather. 'What did you do that for?' gasped Polly. She looked over. 'Who are those two men?'

Kirsty turned furiously back to her. 'Dinna pretend ye canna recognise English Redcoats when ye see them, even at this distance.'

'English?' said Polly. She started to rise. 'That's all right, then, we're safe.'

Kirsty pulled her back down beside her. 'Do you want to get us both killed . . . and worse!'

'I don't understand.'

'Look,' said Kirsty. 'Look through this.' She handed the telescope to Polly. 'They're going to hang our men.'

Polly took the spyglass from her and looked through. The soldiers were placing the rope around Colin's neck. In line were Jamie, the Doctor, and Ben, each bound. 'You're right,' said Polly. 'It's horrible. Can't they be stopped?'

30

Kirsty looked at her in tears. 'How?'

Polly shook her head. 'I dunno, there must be something we can do.'

Kirsty, used to the more passive ways of 18th century women, shook her head in resigned sorrow. 'We can but mourn.' She started to weep.

Polly, an independent girl from the sixties, shrugged her shoulders in disgust. 'You're a weeping ninny. You've still got breath to run, haven't you?'

Kirsty looked up, nodding. Something in the other girl's tone gave her fresh hope.

'Then,' said Polly, 'let's create a diversion, shall we?' She looked around her and picked up a stone. Then, running forward down the path a little way, she flung it as hard as she could towards the group around the cottage. The stone fell just short of them, and the men looked around towards the two girls.

.

'Look, sir,' Klegg grasped Lieutenant Algernon Ffinch's arm. 'Away on that hill there.'

Algernon shaded his eyes and stared. 'It looks like a wench,' he said. 'And demme, there's another one,' as Kirsty got up and ran out beside Polly, also waving her arms and gesticulating, shaking her fists down at the group of British soldiers.

'Puts me in mind of what Sergeant King of the Dragoons said, sir.'

'Uhh?' Algernon didn't follow the Sergeant.

'The Dragoons have orders to stop every woman, sir. Not that they need orders like that, of course,' he said with the hint of a smile.

'Get to the point, Sergeant,' Algernon said crisply.

'Sorry, sir. The thing is, they've heard the Prince is trying to escape disguised as a girl.' He turned back to look at the two figures on the hill. 'Shall I go after them, sir?'

Algernon thought for a moment and shook his head.

'No, Sergeant, you stay here, I'll go.' He turned and beckoned to two of the Redcoats. 'You two men come with me.' The Lieutenant, followed by the two soldiers, strode up the hill towards the girls. Behind them, the Doctor and Ben had noticed the two.

'That looks like Polly and that Scots girl,' Ben whispered to the Doctor.

'Keep quiet about it,' the Doctor returned. 'They're trying to create a diversion.'

'A what?' Ben began, then seeing the Doctor's gaze he closed his mouth.

Polly and Kirsty made sure that they were being followed, and then Polly turned to Kirsty.

'This is our chance,' she said. 'That officer's coming after us. They can't hang them with the officer away. Time to go, fast.'

Kirsty shook her head. 'It'll do nay good.'

'Rubbish. You must know the moors better than they do.'

Kirsty thought for a moment, then nodded. 'Aye, there is a track.'

'Good,' said Polly, 'then let's take it. Come on, girl! We're younger than they are. They'll never catch us.' They turned and began scrambling along a narrow cow track indicated by Kirsty. Behind them, Algernon and the soldiers also burst into a trot, sweating in their heavy uniforms, and obviously no match for the agile girls.

'Vat a great devotion to duty your Lieutenant shows, Sergeant,' said the Doctor.

The Sergeant turned cynically to look at the Doctor. 'Devotion to duty my . . . ' he laughed. 'Devotion to the £30,000 reward for the capture of Prince Charlie, that's what he's after.'

The Doctor raised his eyebrows. 'You think he'll catch them then?'

The Sergeant spat. 'That young whelp? He couldn't catch his own grandmother.' A couple of the soldiers standing by caught his words and laughed, but the Sergeant turned and stiffened them back to attention with a fierce glare.

The Doctor clicked his tongue in disapproval, sensing an opportunity. 'Ach! Sergeant. Disrespect to your superior officer. I could report you for that, you know.'

The Sergeant smiled at him. 'Yeah, you could, but you won't.'

'Perhaps,' said the Doctor, 'I vill, and perhaps I von't. But, at a price.'

'Never mind the price,' said the Sergeant. 'You won't, because you won't be here when he gets back.' He turned to the soldiers. 'Right, proceed with the hanging, you scum.' He looked at Colin who had now slumped down unconscious, and then turned and pointed at Ben. 'We'll start with that ruffian.'

The soldiers took the rope from around Colin's neck and, dragging the protesting Ben over to the tree, made it fast around his neck.

'Hey,' said Ben, 'you can't hang us with your officer away. It ain't proper.'

The Sergeant shrugged his shoulders and brought out a small clay pipe which he proceeded to fill with tobacco. 'Why do you think he went away? Delicate stomach, he has. Always leaves the dirty stuff to others like me.' He turned to the soldiers. 'Right,' he called 'haul him up.'

The soldiers bunched around the rope and began pulling it taut.

'Take the strain,' said the Sergeant. 'Stand by.' He raised his hand, and Ben, now on tiptoes, felt the rope tighten around his neck. 'Ready,' said the Sergeant.

Just then, Solicitor Grey strode around the corner of the cottage, followed by Perkins. 'One moment,' he called. He came over, brought out a lorgnette and looked Ben over carefully.

'Who the devil may you be?' asked the Sergeant.

Grey ignored him and finished his examination of Ben. 'Perkins,' he called over his shoulder.

Perkins reached in his pocket and pulled out a large parchment commission sealed with a red seal. He handed it to the Sergeant. 'This,' he said importantly, 'is Solicitor Grey of Lincolns Inn Fields, his Majesty's Commissioner for the disposal of rebel prisoners.'

The Sergeant took the commission a little suspiciously and looked at it, holding it upside down. He obviously was unable to read.

The Doctor, stretching his bound hands, leaned over and took it from him, looking at it. 'Perhaps I can help,' he said.

Grey turned to the soldiers. 'Take the noose off and set this young man down.'

'Set him down,' echoed Perkins, who had a habit of repeating his master's orders.

The soldiers paused irresolutely, looking from Grey to the Sergeant. The Sergeant, his authority challenged, flushed angrily.

'I don't care who you are,' he said, 'you've no charge over my men.'

Grey turned, his voice a whiplash. 'Can you not read, Sergeant? I have charge over all rebel prisoners, and you and your men are ordered to give me every assistance.'

'Of course he has,' Perkins burst in self-importantly. 'Appointed by the Chief Justice of England, Mr Grey is. All prisoners,' he repeated.

The Sergeant turned uncertainly and started blustering. 'Not these, he ain't!'

Grey looked at him for a moment, then turned back to Perkins. 'Perkins,' he said, 'the other pocket, I think.' Perkins nodded, felt in a pocket, and brought out a handful of silver coins which he proceeded to count out from one hand to the other. Grey turned back to the Sergeant.

34

'I admit a prior claim, Sergeant, but I think you are a reasonable man.' The Sergeant was watching the coins. A sergeant's pay at that time was five shillings a week. He watched, fascinated, as Perkins counted out ten silver coins, then stopped.

'I'm not sure,' he said as Perkins looked up at him.

'Continue, Perkins,' instructed Grey. Perkins shrugged his shoulders a little unwillingly, and began to count out another handful.

'Of course, I regret any trouble,' continued Grey, 'encountered by you and' – indicating the other soldiers – 'these fine fellows. But if this will help . . .' Perkins finished counting out a handful of silver coins and held it toward the Sergeant.

The Sergeant nodded, took the money and placed it in a pouch hanging at his belt. He turned back to his men. 'You heard the Commissioner, get him down smart like.' The men took the noose from Ben's neck and released him.

Ben turned to the Solicitor. 'Phew, that feels better. Thanks a lot, mate.'

Grey gave him a slight bow. 'A trifle, I assure you.' He reached in and took out a snuffbox, delicately taking a small pinch of snuff between finger and thumb and sniffing it. He gave a dainty sneeze, and then continued. 'Strong ruffians like you and' – he looked at the other three and nodded towards Jamie – 'this young rebel here are needed at His Majesty's colonies.' He turned to look at the wounded Laird. 'You can dispatch this one, Sergeant, and' – he turned and raised his lorgnette to look at the Doctor – 'this strange looking scoundrel here.'

Perkins snatched the commission from the Doctor's hand. The Doctor gave a slight bow. 'Article XVII, Aliens Act 1730,' he said.

'Pardon?' asked Grey.

'Ah, I thought you vere a gentleman of the law.'

Perkins elbowed him back. 'How dare you speak to Mr Grey like that.'

Grey gave a slight smile, amused. 'I am a lawyer.'

'Then you are doubtless familiar with Article XVII,' said the Doctor. 'You cannot hang a citizen of a foreign power vithout notifying his ambassador.'

Perkins, puzzled, raised his tatty grey wig and started scratching his scalp. 'Article XVII . . . Aliens?'

Grey turned to the Sergeant. 'Who is this extraordinary rogue?'

The Sergeant shrugged his shoulders. 'Claims to be a frog doctor, sir.'

'No, German,' corrected the Doctor. 'And better acquainted vith the English law than you seem to be, Solicitor.'

The Sergeant pushed the Doctor back. 'I'm the only law that matters to you now, matey, and if this gentleman don't want you, you hang. All right, lads.' The men raised the noose for the Doctor, but Grey raised his hand.

'Wait,' he said. He turned to the Doctor. 'You show a touching faith in His Majesty's justice, sir, and a doctor, too. Well . . . we need doctors in the plantations. You can send him along with the other prisoners, Sergeant, to Inverness.'

Jamie spoke for the first time. 'What about the Laird?' Grey turned to him. Jamie pointed to the wounded Colin. 'The Laird McLaren. Either the Laird goes wi' us or you can hang me right here. I'll no go without him.'

'Ho,' said the Sergeant, 'we'll see about that.'

'Sergeant,' Grey restrained him. He turned to the Doctor. 'What do you think, Doctor? Can this man be healed of his wound?' He indicated Colin.

The Doctor nodded. 'With proper care.'

Grey took another pinch of snuff. 'Whether he'll get that where he's going is somewhat doubtful, but I'll leave him in your care. Send them all to Inverness, Sergeant.'

'Right sir. *Shun!*' The men came to attention.

'Corporal!' barked the Sergeant. One of the bigger of the soldiers shuffled forward and saluted. 'You accompany this gentleman' – he indicated Grey – 'and the prisoners to Inverness. I'll wait here for Lieutenant Ffinch.'

'Where's that you're taking us?' asked Ben, looking anxiously at the Doctor. He realised the danger of being separated too far from the TARDIS, their one hope of getting back to his own time.

'To Inverness,' said Grey, 'to start with. Then perhaps a sea voyage. Say . . . three thousand miles?' He smiled at them: a slow, sinister smile.

'Three thousand miles?' said Ben. The soldiers formed a group around the Doctor, Ben and Jamie and, lifting the wounded Laird between two of them, set off across the moor. The Sergeant refilled his pipe and sat down in front of the cottage, waiting for his officer's return.

5

Polly and Kirsty

Polly, walking barefoot and carrying her thin shoes in her hand, stumbled after Kirsty, the fleet-footed Highland lass. Kirsty was leading her through another part of the moor towards higher ground. Around them were tall outcrops of rock, some as large as a house with great splits and fissures big enough to hide a man. Kirsty made for one, and when Polly looked up from rubbing her leg, scratched for the twentieth time that day, her companion had disappeared.

But she had no time to panic before Kirsty suddenly emerged from a slender fissure of rock. 'Whist,' she called. 'Do you want to draw them over here?' Polly came over curiously.

'Oh,' she said, 'we're miles ahead of them now. They'll never catch up with us. What have you found?'

'It's a cave,' said Kirsty, 'I'll show you.' She led Polly through the rock fissure, sliding agilely around a slight bend, and Polly, to her astonishment, found herself in a large cave worn from the interior of the rock by a small stream. In one corner, away from the fissure which ran up twenty feet and showed a thin strip of grey sky, there were blankets and a rough cot, and several old chests.

'You don't mean to say you live here,' exclaimed Polly, turning to Kirsty.

Kirsty turned angrily on the other girl. 'You think we live in caves?'

'I'm sorry,' muttered Polly.

'Nay,' said Kirsty. 'My clan use it as a hide-out after cattle raids.'

'Cattle raids?' said Polly. 'You mean, you steal people's cattle?'

Kirsty, startled, stood back. 'Och, no! What do you take us for? We're no thieves. We only steal from those who take from us . . . like the McGregor clan.' Kirsty walked forward and opened the nearest of the small wooden chests. 'We keep our food in here.' She looked in it hungrily, and rummaged among some old parchments, then brought up something that to Polly looked suspiciously like a large, hard dog biscuit. 'Och,' said Kirsty, 'we've only one wee biscuit left. The men must have got here before us.'

Polly looked suspiciously down at the biscuit. 'When was it left here?'

'About three months past,' said Kirsty, and started gnawing hungrily on a corner of the biscuit. Then, remembering her manners, she offered it to the stranger. Polly wrinkled her nose in disgust and shook her head.

'Ugh,' she said, 'dog biscuits!'

Kirsty looked up, annoyed. 'Biscuits are no bait for dogs,' she said, and set to work on it.

'Well, not for me,' said Polly, 'please go ahead. I don't want to lose my fillings.'

Kirsty looked blankly up at her.

'Oh, teeth, you know . . . fillings, teeth. Never mind, I'm not hungry. We must make a plan. We saw them being marched away; now, where would they be taking them?'

Kirsty burst into tears. 'To Inverness gaol. They'll never leave that place alive.'

Polly looked down at the dishevelled, weeping girl, annoyed. 'Oh don't be such a wet. We must get them out. Have you any money?'

Kirsty looked up, shaking her head. 'For what do we need money?'

'For food, of course,' Polly returned. 'That biscuit won't last us long, and we need something to bribe the guards with. What have we got to sell then?' Polly looked down at her bracelet, which was of twisted silver. She shook it. 'This won't fetch much, but it's a start, anyway.'

'Why would you help us?' said Kirsty. 'You are English, you're not one of us.'

'They've got my friends, too, remember,' Polly rejoined. She shivered. The air in the cave was chill and damp. 'And I must get myself some proper clothes to wear.'

'Aye,' said Kirsty curiously, her tears forgotten. 'Why do you wear the short skirts of a bairn? Ye're a grown woman sure.'

Polly looked down at her mini-skirt and the torn and laddered tights. 'Well,' said Polly, 'you see . . . Oh, it'll take too long to explain.' She looked over at Kirsty and spotted a large ring on the girl's middle finger. 'Ah,' she said, 'that ring, it's gold.'

Kirsty immediately covered the ring with her other hand and turned away.

'Oh come on,' said Polly crossly, 'can't I even look at it? You'll have to trust me, you know.'

Kirsty shook her head. 'It's no mine, it's my father's.'

'Well let's see anyway.'

Kirsty reluctantly stretched her hand out and Polly examined the ring. 'Oh, it's a gorgeous seal. We should get a lot for that.'

Kirsty snatched her hand back and looked up, frightened. 'We're no selling it.'

Polly stared back at her in disbelief. 'Not even to save your father's life?'

'No.' Kirsty shook her head firmly. 'He'd no thank me.'

Polly shrugged her shoulders. 'Oh, you're hopeless. Why, for goodness sake?'

'He entrusted it to me before the battle. He'd kill me if I ever parted with it.'

'I don't understand you people,' Polly sighed. Then with sudden resolution she held her hand out. 'Come on,' she said, 'give it to me.'

Kirsty scrabbled away across the floor, reached out and grabbed the dirk that Polly had been wearing and had set down on one of the chests. 'I will not!' she said.

Polly stared at her for a moment, and then shook her head in disgust. 'Keep your ring,' she said, 'you're just a wild wailing peasant. I'm off to help my companions. You just stay here and guard your precious ring.' She turned back towards the door.

Kirsty looked up, anxious now that her one companion was leaving. 'Och, mind your step outside, it'll be dark soon.'

'Oh, watch out for yourself,' Polly shot back, annoyed, as she exited.

Kirsty stood up, calling after her. 'You'll get lost for sure.' But Polly was already out of earshot.

Outside the cave it was indeed getting dark. The moor, which had seemed harmless enough in the daylight, now took on a totally different aspect, full of mysterious shapes that loomed up at Polly. She stared to retrace her footsteps back towards the cottage. At all costs she must find out what had happened to the Doctor and Ben. Even if the English soldiers captured her, what could they do? They surely wouldn't harm an English girl, she reflected. Anyway, she didn't doubt her ability to talk her way out of any situation – *What was that?*

Polly whipped around. She'd heard a noise, a stone rattling away down the slope not far behind her. Somebody was following her, or was it some animal or . . . For the first time Polly began believing the stories of witches, warlocks, and hobgoblins which so scared the eighteenth century Kirsty. Polly looked around. Beside the road there was a short, thick stick. She picked it up and held it out as a club. 'Who's there?' she called, but there was no answer and the scuffling noises seemed to have stopped.

The night seemed even darker now, and for a moment Polly thought of going back to the cave; but that would have meant admitting to Kirsty that she was scared, and a silly weeping ninny like her – no, this she could never do. She moved forward again along the rough track, with her head slightly turned and her ear cocked, listening for more tell-tale noises. She didn't notice that the path had branched and she was following a smaller path rather than the main track. Then Polly thought she heard another noise behind her, this time the crack of a twig. She began to run along the track, really scared this time.

Suddenly, the ground beneath her feet seemed to disappear, and she found herself falling down through the darkness.

Polly screamed, and clutched at some grass verging what was obviously some sort of animal trap or pit; but the grass did not hold her. The clump slowly pulled out, and she slid down to the bottom of the trap, winded, dirty and very much afraid.

For a couple of minutes, Polly lay still, hardly daring to move, afraid of where she had fallen. Might there not be some wild animal beside her in this pit? She tried to remember whether they still had wolves in Scotland in the eighteenth century, or even – she shivered at the thought – bears!

However, all she could hear were the usual night sounds, the distant shriek of an owl hunting its prey, the rustle of the wind in the trees just beyond the pit, and her own gradually subsiding panting. She stood up and felt her arms and legs, but beyond one or two bruises and some thick-caked dirt, there seemed to be no damage. She felt her way around the edges of the pit. It was about ten foot deep and six foot square at the bottom, but some of the sides had caved in, and Polly began scrambling up the loose earth. As she neared the surface, she could make out a latticework of branches, some fairly thick and strong, covering the other end of the pit from where she had fallen through. One of them looked strong enough to stand her weight, and with a great effort she leapt up and managed to hold onto it. She pulled her other hand up and then started pulling her way along the branch to heave herself out of the pit, when a hand came into view and shoved the branch back into the pit. Down Polly scrambled. As she looked up, she saw that the hand was now extended over her head, and was holding a dagger.

6

Polly's Prisoner

As Polly looked up, the hand that held the dagger seemed to be raising it as if to fling it right down at the helpless girl beneath.

'Don't,' cried Polly, 'please, I give up!'

There was a scuffle of leaves above her and then Kirsty's head appeared over the edge of the pit. 'It's your self!' she exclaimed. The Scottish girl was so startled she dropped the dagger. Polly, with a quick twist, managed to turn away as it stuck into the ground beside her.

'Careful, you idiot!' shouted Polly. Then, angry because she'd been so afraid, said crossly 'Of course it's my self—who did you think it was?'

'Och, I'm sorry,' said Kirsty. 'I thought maybe a Redcoat had fallen into the animal trap—and I wish it had been.'

'It's lucky for both of us that it didn't happen that way. Come on, help me get out of here,' said Polly.

'Give me your hand.' Kirsty stretched her arm over, and Polly scrambled up towards Kirsty's hand. She grabbed it, but the Scots girl had not balanced herself on the edge, and Polly, the bigger girl, pulled her back over, so the both of them tumbled once more to the bottom of the pit.

'Oh, help,' said Polly, 'are you hurt?'

Kirsty sat up and started brushing the earth off her arms. 'No', she said. 'A wee bruise or two, and a lot of dirt. Och, but now we're both trapped,' she wailed.

'Not on your nelly,' said Polly. 'Even you Scottish lasses must've played piggy-back at some time.'

'I dinna understand.'

'You get down,' Polly said, 'I climb on your back and scramble up, then I'll pull you up.'

'Oh, I ken,' said Kirsty. She kneeled; Polly got on her back and climbed up, raising her head above the level of the pit, and started reaching for a good hand-hold to pull herself out. She stopped and stared. A light was approaching along the path.

'Quick wi' ye,' Kirsty's voice came from below. 'You're no light weight, you know.'

Polly turned and looked down. 'Shush,' she said, 'there's a light.'

She now made the light out to be a lantern held by an approaching soldier. Behind him was a single file of men. 'It's soldiers,' she called down. She jumped down from Kirsty's back.

'Redcoats!' said Kirsty. 'Och, we're cornered now.'

Polly shook her head. 'Shhh, let's just wait. They'll soon move off. Listen now.'

Up above them, a very weary Lieutenant Algernon Ffinch was stumbling along, leaning on one of his men, with another proceeding with the lantern. It had been a long hike through the mountains, and Algernon's high-heeled elegant London-made boots were not up to the rugged Scottish moors. One heel had come off, and he was lame, cross and very tired. Suddenly, the man who was supporting the Lieutenant stumbled, and Ffinch fell forward.

'You clumsy fool!' he shouted. 'What did you do that for?'

'Sorry, sir,' said the man. 'I think it's some sort of wall.' The soldier with the lantern turned back and revealed the remnants of a low stone wall used to separate the farmers' sheep fields, now in obvious disrepair.

Algernon sat gingerly on the stone wall, and the two men hovered uncertainly above him. Algernon was in a flaming temper.

'Couldn't catch two wenches, could you? Call yourselves "His Majesty's soldiers"? The terror of the Highlands? You wouldn't frighten a one-armed dairymaid. Here'—he turned to the man who'd been supporting him—'pull this boot off.' The soldier leant down, and as he held the boot, Algernon pushed against his shoulder, sending him over backwards with the boot. 'Ah, that's better,' said Algernon. 'I've done enough walking for one day. You two go and fetch my horse. And if you're not back in an hour, six lashes apiece. Do we understand each other?' The frightened soldiers saluted. 'Well, what are you waiting for?' said Algernon. 'Go!' The men turned and started back along the path.

'Imbeciles!' Algernon screamed after them. 'Leave the lantern here. You think I want to be left in the dark?' The soldier with the lantern brought it over and placed it by Algernon. 'Right! Now, quick march!' The soldiers turned and scurried away down the path.

The two girls crouching in the pit heard every word. Kirsty whispered in Polly's ear. 'He's staying there. Now what can we do?' Again, her eyes filled with tears.

Polly gave an exasperated sigh. 'Oh, not again. Didn't the women of your age do anything but cry?' she whispered.

'Aye?' said Kirsty, completely uncomprehending.

But Polly wasn't about to enlighten her on the difference between a girl from the eighteenth century and a girl from the twentieth century.

'Never mind,' she whispered, 'I've got an idea. Now listen. Since our officer has so obligingly parked himself outside our pit, let's lure him to join us down here.'

'Oh no,' said Kirsty, but Polly picked up the dirk and handed it to her. 'You're better with this thing than I

46

am, and we can handle him between us. Now, here's what we can do.'

Above them Algernon was making himself as comfortable as the night and the damp air would permit. He had opened a pouch left by the soldiers containing bread, a chicken leg, and onions. Now he raised the chicken leg and was about to bite into it when he heard a low moan from the pit, rising to a wail and then slowly dying away. The sound was high-pitched and eerie in the extreme. Algernon dropped the chicken leg back into the pouch and reached for his sword hilt. He raised the lantern and looked fiercely around him.

As Algernon did so, another wail arose. Raising the lantern, Algernon quickly established that this ghost-like wail was coming from just behind the wall. His hand shook, but he stood up. He was, after all, an English officer and not supposed to be afraid of ghosties and ghoulies and things that go bump in the night. He drew his sword, holding the lantern out, and scrambled over the wall just as a third wail of a slightly different timbre started up and then cut off abruptly in mid-sound. It appeared to come from a clump of trees beyond a rough patch of ground. (Algernon could not see the gaping hole left by Polly as the other end of the pit was still covered by a cunningly designed matting of branches and grass stalks.) He put his foot on a clump of grass and crashed through into the pit, lantern and all.

The fall completely knocked the wind out of him, and for a moment all he could see was stars. Then he felt the cold steel of a knife held along his throat, and when he opened his eyes he saw before him a strange girl, dressed in a costume that the prim Englishman would have found immodest on a girl of six, never mind a fully grown wench, as he put it to himself, of nearly twenty.

A low Scottish voice hissed in his ear. 'Move and I'll slit your throat from ear to ear.'

47

Algernon tried to move but felt the cold steel pressed deeper against his throat.

'She will, too,' said the strange girl, 'so you'd better keep still. Here.' Polly unbuckled and pulled off his sword belt, then wrapped it tightly around his legs. 'Use the strap for his wrist,' she said to Kirsty. Between them the girls trussed up the fuming young officer.

'Do you know that for assaulting a King's officer . . .' Algernon spluttered.

'I know,' said Polly, 'thirty lashes. But you're not in charge now. We are. Kirsty,' she said, 'turn out his pockets.'

Kirsty, a little shocked, started back. 'Ach, no, I couldna do that.'

'Why not,' said Polly, 'he has money, and we need it.'

'By gad!' Algernon burst out. 'You cannot mean to rob me.'

At his words, Kirsty overcame her scruples. 'And why not?' she said. 'You and your kind have robbed our glens.' She opened his pouch. 'He has food, look . . . chicken, bread.'

'Great,' said Polly. 'Now, my gallant gentleman, your pockets.'

'I have done you no harm . . .' began Algernon.

'No harm!' said Kirsty. 'It is no thanks to you that my father and Jamie were not hanged. They're probably rotting in Inverness gaol by now.' She felt in his pocket and brought her hand out. Then reacted in wide-eyed incredulity. 'Will you look at this?' she cried.

As Polly bent forward to look, she saw in Kirsty's hand the gleam of golden guineas.

7

The Water Dungeon

'Right old rathole this is,' said Ben. Ben, the Doctor, Jamie and Colin were in a circular cell, like a medieval dungeon. Colin, still only half conscious, was propped up on two steps that led down to the floor cell, behind him the strong oak door with a narrow-barred grille. The walls oozed damp, and were covered with green moss. As Ben looked down, he saw that water was beginning to seep in through cracks in the rough stone walls. Illumination came from a spluttering tar torch stuck in a bracket beside the door. As they looked up, they could see an iron grille, and through it the white gaiters of the English sentry. Jamie was sitting on the step beside the Laird, and the Doctor was stretched out on a rough stone bench built against the wall, his legs out, seemingly unconcerned with his surroundings.

Jamie looked over at Ben. 'If you think this is a rathole, King George has worse to offer, never fear.'

'Yeah, I reckon you're right,' said Ben. 'I'm glad, at least, that Polly's out of this. I wonder if she's all right.' The last remark was directed at the Doctor, who didn't seem to have heard, lost in his own thoughts, and humming gently to himself.

'Doctor,' said Ben. 'Doctor.'

The Doctor looked at him. 'I expect she's all right,' he said, 'she got away.'

'Why did we ever get mixed up with this lot?' said Ben.

'Well,' said the Doctor, 'it wasn't exactly my idea.' Then, as he saw Ben's face fall, he went on, 'Oh, don't worry, I'm rather glad we did. It's quite an adventure. I'm just beginning to enjoy myself.'

Then, as Ben raised his eyes heavenward – he would never understand the Doctor no matter how long he spent in his company – the Doctor continued, 'I bet this place has an echo. It's a classic shape. Let's try, shall we?' He put his hands beside his mouth and at the top of his voice yelled, 'Down with King George!' His voice, picked up by the circular room, produced an echo that took several seconds to die down. 'There,' said the Doctor, satisfied, 'I'm right.'

'Silence, you Jacobite pigs! Unless you want a touch of this bayonet,' the sentry called.

Jamie turned round to the Doctor, wide-eyed. 'So you are for the Prince after all?'

'Oh, not really,' the Doctor shrugged. 'I just like listening to the echo. Well, to work,' he said. He went over to Colin. 'Let's have another look at that wound, shall we?' He started to pull Colin's plaid aside to look at the shoulder wound.

'Will you be letting him now?' said Jamie.

'Oh, I don't think so,' said the Doctor. 'With rest it should heal.'

'Heal!' Jamie was outraged. 'And you claim to be a doctor? You've no bled him yet.'

''Ere,' Ben intervened, 'what's he on about?'

'Blood-letting,' said the Doctor.

'But that's daft.'

'It is the only method of curing the sick,' said Jamie.

'Huh,' Ben scoffed. 'Killing them, more like. He's lost enough blood already, don't you think.'

The Doctor felt in his pocket and brought up a small telescope, then turned it upwards to where a few pale stars were visible through the grille. He began muttering to himself. 'Oh Isis and Osiris, is it meet?'

'Oh no,' said Ben. 'What are you on about now?'

'Whist, man.' Jamie was impressed.

The Doctor took another look through the telescope. 'Gemini in Taurus.' He turned abruptly to Jamie. 'When was the Laird born?'

'In the fifth month,' said Jamie.

'Ah,' said the Doctor, 'that's what I thought. The blood-letting must wait until Taurus is in the ascendant. So it is willed.'

'Stone a crow!' said Ben. 'You don't believe in all that codswallop, do you Doctor?'

'Of course I do,' said the Doctor. He gave Ben a quick wink and nodded over his shoulder. 'So does he. And he's never heard of germs.'

Jamie looked puzzled. 'What was that word?'

'Oh,' said the Doctor, 'germs, they're all around us.'

Jamie reacted at this a little fearfully, shrinking back and looking round him as if he expected to see germs hopping off the walls.

'Have you a handkerchief, Ben?' said the Doctor.

'Uh, I think so. It's not too clean,' said Ben. He pulled out a small pocket handkerchief.

Jamie looked at it in disgust. 'That wee lass's handkerchief? Here Doctor, try mine.' Jamie felt inside his shirt and pulled out a great square of linen giving it to the Doctor, who began binding Colin's wound. As he did so, he noticed the corner of a silken object protruding from underneath the Laird's bulky plaid.

'Ah, what've we got here?' said the Doctor. 'Ben, give me a hand.' Together they unwrapped Colin's plaid and pulled out a large, square silk standard, heavily embroidered and ornate, with silken tassels. The Doctor held it up. 'What have we here?'

Jamie's eyes almost started out of his head. 'It's – It's, aye, Prince Charlie's personal standard.'

'Then what's he doing with it?' Ben pointed to the Laird.

51

'Protecting it. Now put it back, will ye. If the English find it –'

'Ah, wait.' The Doctor took it, opened his coat, and wrapped it around his body, then buttoned his coat again. The floppy, disreputable frock coat the Doctor wore looked little different for the addition.

Jamie started forward angrily. 'What do you think you're doing?'

The Doctor pointed at Colin. 'And what chance do you think he'll stand of evading the gallows with this on him?'

Jamie stood nonplussed, scratching his head. 'Och, well –'

'Besides, it'll keep me warm. Now Jamie,' he said, 'play us a tune to cheer us up.'

Jamie felt inside his coat and brought out the playing pipe of a set of bagpipes – all he had managed to salvage from his piper's equipment after the battle. 'Here,' he said, 'I'll do mah best, but I canna do real justice to a tune without a bag and pipes ye ken.' He started to blow a sad, soft, plaintive little Highland tune on the pipe. Soft as it was, it carried to the ears of the sentry above them.

'Stop that noise!' he called down.

Ben, whose taste in music leant more towards rock and pop, turned to Jamie. 'Do you call that cheering us up?'

Jamie looked wounded, and the Doctor gently put his hand on his shoulder. 'What Ben means, I think, is that he'd like to hear something a little more cheerful. I'm rather good at this sort of thing myself. May I try?'

Ben groaned and turned away, holding his head. 'Here we go,' he said. The one thing they always suffered from on this and other trips was the Doctor's musical efforts.

Jamie drew himself up a little proudly. 'You'll not be able to play it, you know. It takes a McCrimmon to play the pipes.'

'Well, never mind,' the Doctor shrugged. He felt in his

pocket and brought out the tin whistle he always carried in an inside pocket. Then, playing loudly and a little shrilly, he fingered the jaunty tune 'Lillibulero', the Jacobite marching song.

Even Jamie was alarmed at this. 'Eee,' he said, 'whist ye!'

The Doctor stopped playing for a moment. 'You're a loyal Jacobite, aren't you? This is your song. Ben, whistle it with me. Come on.'

As the Doctor led them, Jamie, looking around a little nervously, and Ben, not in the least comprehending the significance of the tune, started to whistle the catchy rhythms of the march. Up above them, the sentry, a loyal follower of King George, to whom the tune of 'Lillibulero' was the very symbol of the rebellion which had so nearly conquered Great Britain, pointed the musket down through the grille. 'Silence, I say,' he said. 'I've warned you rebels once.'

The Doctor played louder, and over by the door Colin opened his eyes and smiled faintly at the sound of the rallying song of the Jacobite army.

'All right,' said the soldier, 'we'll see if a touch of this bayonet will hush ye.' He turned and ran towards the staircase leading down to the cell.

The Doctor immediately stopped playing and passed Jamie back his pipe. 'I think this is yours,' he said.

A moment later, the long bolts rattled back and the door was flung open. The sentry glared around at them. 'Who's responsible for this?' he cried.

The Doctor immediately stepped forward. To Ben's surprise he was putting on his German accent again.

'Ach, himmel,' he said, 'did you hear that tune?'

The sentry nodded suspiciously. 'The rebel dirge.' He looked at the Doctor. 'And you were playing it.'

'Ach, nein. They were playing it. To drive me out of my mind.' He placed his hand on his heart. 'I am from Hanover, a loyal subject of King George the Second.'

53

The sentry scowled at him suspiciously. 'What's that to do with me?'

The Doctor looked back at the others. Ben realised that the Doctor was up to some ruse, but Jamie was completely outraged by this latest switch in the Doctor's shifting loyalties.

'They know the plan to murder your general, the Duke of Cumberland,' said the Doctor.

'That's a lie!' Jamie burst out. Jamie turned round to Colin who was now sitting up and taking notice. 'I knew he was no one of us,' he said.

'Well,' said the sentry truculently, still looking rather suspiciously at the Doctor.

'Take me to Commissioner Grey, and let us hope we may be in time to stop it.'

'Why did you not speak before?' said the sentry, still suspicious.

'Ach,' said the Doctor, ''tis just discovered.' He pointed at Jamie. 'And that rogue is a party to it.'

This was too much for Jamie. He flung himself forward to throttle the Doctor, but the sentry intercepted him with a bayonet levelled at his chest. 'Ye filthy spy, ye,' said Jamie, furious.

Ben grabbed hold of Jamie's arm and pulled him back. This finally convinced the sentry that the Doctor was sincere: Jamie's anger was too intense to be anything but the real thing. He nodded behind him. 'Go on,' he said, 'out!'

The Doctor gave a quick wink at Ben, and then walked out of the door. The sentry backed out and slammed the door behind them.

Ben nodded approvingly at Jamie. 'Well done, mate,' he said.

Jamie was still furious. 'What d'you mean, and why dinna ye join your friend with the other traitors?'

'Aw, calm down,' said Ben. 'Can't you see it was all a fiddle?'

'Fiddle?' said Jamie.

'Trick, mate. A ruse, to get us out of here.'

Jamie shook his head, trying to comprehend. 'I dinna understand ye.'

Ben shook his head, then patiently tried to explain. 'Blimey, listen. Outside, he's got a chance to get away and get help, to rescue us. What chance do you think he's got paddling around in here?' He looked down to where the water was now lapping around their feet.

Jamie finally seemed to comprehend what Ben was saying. 'Aye,' he said, 'I see. But nevertheless, I'm a' worriet.'

Ben looked around the cell. 'Well, don't waste time worrying about the Doctor, mate. Worry about us.' He pointed up to a dark line which ran all the way around the circular cell. 'That's a tide mark, unless I'm very much mistaken.' He bent down and tasted the water. 'Yeah, salt. 'Ere,' he touched the mark which was some foot above their heads. 'That's where the water level comes up to when the tide's in, and it ain't my bath night.'

8

Blackmail

In the lantern light, Polly was carefully counting out Algernon's money. 'Eighteen, nineteen, twenty guineas. Hmm . . . how far will that get us, do you think?'

Kirsty, beside her, was wide-eyed. 'I've never seen so much money in all my days,' she said.

'You'll both h-hang for this, you know,' said Algernon.

Polly turned to him. 'You're very fond of hanging, Mr uh-h-h . . .' She had an idea. 'Here, what is your name?'

Algernon set his mouth and turned his face away. 'I refuse to tell you.'

'Oh, we're very brave all of a sudden, aren't we?' said Polly. She turned to Kirsty. 'He must have some identification on him. Let's find it.' Polly leaned forward and unbuttoned the top of Algernon's waistcoat. Underneath, there was a large crescent-shaped identity disc, worn by all the British soldiers of that period. She pulled it out towards the light and read, 'Algernon Thomas Alfred Ff' – she stumbled for a moment on his surname – 'Ffinch. With two "f"s yet? A Lieutenant in the Honourable Colonel Atwood's Rifles.' She laughed. 'I'll bet the Honourable Colonel Atwood would be interested to hear how one of his lieutenants was captured by two weak girls.'

For the first time, Algernon's eyes widened in fear. 'Oh come,' he said, 'surely you would not tell . . .'

Polly smiled at him. 'Oh, wouldn't we, Algernon.' She turned to Kirsty. 'Give me that knife.'

Kirsty handed over the dirk.

Algernon braced himself. 'What are you going to do?' he said.

'Never fear, Algernon Thomas Alfred,' said Polly. She cut off a lock of his hair protruding from under the dishevelled white wig. 'You know,' said Polly, 'how girls like souvenirs of their fellows.' She looked at him. 'Well, perhaps you don't, but I'm just after a small souvenir of you. There.' She then raised the dirk and cut the cord that held the identity disc. 'This hair should be proof enough that we captured you. Just in case the Colonel doesn't believe us.'

Kirsty had been watching this with astonishment. 'But why would you be . . .'

Polly turned to her. 'We may need an ally in the enemy camp.' She looked back at the unhappy Algernon. 'And I think we've found one.' She nudged him with the dirk. 'Right, Algernon?'

'It's sheer b-b-blackmail,' sputtered Algernon.

'You got that one right,' said Polly, 'that's what it is.' She turned. 'Come on, Kirsty, we'd better get out of here before his men get back. Sit up, Algy dear.' Polly helped Algernon to a sitting position then, standing lightly on his knee and shoulder, she swung herself gracefully over the top of the pit, then turned and helped Kirsty out the same way.

She looked down at Algernon. 'Don't worry, they won't be long, I'm sure. And we'll be looking out for you in Inverness. Don't forget.'

The last thing Algernon heard was Polly's light laugh rippling back as the two girls scampered away down the hillside.

The Sea Eagle was one of the finest inns in the town of Inverness. It had been built largely for the occupying English soldiers who had one of their main fortresses at Inverness, and was a large handsome timbered building, unlike the low thick-walled cottages that usually passed for inns in the highlands of Scotland.

Solicitor Grey, his clerk Perkins, and a heavily-built ruffian in seaman's clothes, Henry Trask, was with them.

Captain Trask, as he styled himself, was master of the brig *Annabelle*. A one-time pirate gunrunner and smuggler, Trask's hard nature showed on his face. It was deeply lined with a livid scar running across the forehead, and pock-marked with a blue powder mark left by the unpredictable guns of the period which often blew up in a man's face.

Right now, Trask, who'd obviously been drinking—there was an empty wine bottle on its side in front of him, and a full flagon at his lips—was in a raucous good humour. 'Well, lawyer,' he said, 'my old cattleboat's ready for its livestock. Eh?' He roared with laughter, and Perkins beside him gave a mild, conciliatory titter in reply. The half-drunk Trask, always quick to take offence, stopped laughing immediately and glared at him. 'Belay there.' Perkins's laugh cut off abruptly. 'What in thunder do you think you're laughing at?'

N-n-nothing,' said Perkins, beginning to stammer nervously. But Grey leaned across the table, his face serious.

'It won't be a laughing matter for any of us if we are caught, I assure you. That is why we must start loading the prisoners tonight.'

Beside him, Perkins, relieved to have Trask's attention diverted, nodded and repeated Grey's last words. 'Yes, tonight,' he said.

'By the time the King's judges are ready to try the rebels, we shall have them safely on the plantations,' continued Grey.

Trask leaned forward, nodding his great head. 'Aye,' he said. 'A Highlander will do twice the work of one of your black slaves.'

Perkins smirked. 'At least twice,' he said.

Trask immediately turned on him. 'Who asked for your opinion?'

Perkins, snubbed again, shrank back from the fearsome-looking captain, but Grey interposed and rapped the table with his snuffbox. 'Silence, Captain,' he said. 'I won't have my clerk bullied in this way.'

Then as Trask scowled in his direction, he leaned forward, his eyes searching the seaman's face. 'I have enough evidence on you to send you to the gallows ten times over. Don't forget it.'

For a moment Trask rose in his chair and seemed about to throttle the quiet-spoken lawyer. Then, the steely intensity of the solicitor's unflinching gaze made him uneasy and he slumped back, dropping his eyes and reaching for the wine flagon.

There was a knock at the door. 'Come in,' Grey called. The door opened and the sentry stuck his head round. 'Well?' said Grey.

'It's one of the prisoners, Sir. He insists on seeing you. Says he's got some special information about a plot on the Duke's life.'

'Why come to me?'

'He won't talk to anyone but you, Sir,' said the sentry.

'Which prisoner is it?' said Grey.

'The German doctor, Sir.'

Grey looked puzzled for a moment, and then his face cleared. 'Ah, interesting,' he said. 'Bring him up to me at once.'

The sentry saluted, but made no move to go.

'Well man, what are you waiting for?' Still the sentry stood there immobile, his eyes staring straight ahead. 'Ahh,' Grey sighed and turned to his clerk. 'Perkins,' he said.

Perkins rather reluctantly felt in his waistcoat pocket and brought out two coins. He selected the smaller and gave it to the sentry. The sentry took it and looked at it for a moment in disgust, then exited.

Grey turned back to Trask. 'Now, Captain,' he continued, 'I suggest you start loading the prisoners.' He turned to a small leather case beside him on the table, opened it and brought out an imposing-looking parchment document with ribbons and large seals attached. 'Here is your warrant. To save comment, bring them through the back way.' The door opened, and the Doctor entered, followed by the sentry. Grey looked back at the Captain. 'Right, and you go with him, Perkins.' Trask nodded, rose and, followed by Perkins, walked to the door, watched carefully by the Doctor.

Grey opened the leather case once more and brought out a small, silver-mounted flintlock pistol. He looked at it for a moment and then put it down on the table in front of him, then nodded to the sentry. 'You may go, man.' The sentry saluted and left the room. Grey turned back to the Doctor.

'Now Doctor,' he said. 'Your story. Let us hope it is an entertaining one. It cost me a silver shilling. What is the nature of this plot?'

The Doctor looked at him for a moment and then shrugged and started picking his teeth. 'There is no plot,' he said carelessly.

For a moment Grey looked surprised, then his face darkened. 'Be careful, Doctor, how you waste my time. I can have every inch of skin flayed off your back just by a snap of my fingers.'

The Doctor held his hand up and started examining his nails, speaking casually over his shoulder. 'Would the chance to lay hands on £15,000 be a waste of your time?'

Grey leaned back, faintly amused. '£15,000, you vagabond? Where would you get £15,000?'

For answer, the Doctor glanced around, then opened his coat and started to unwrap the Prince's silk standard from around his waist. Grey snatched up the pistol and

60

levelled it at him, but the Doctor continued unwrapping and then held up the standard, smiling. 'Here we have,' said the Doctor, 'the personal standard of Charles Edward Stuart, Pretender to the throne of England.'

Grey studied it in astonishment. 'Indeed,' he said.

'Whoever was entrusted with the standard stood closest to the council of the Prince, wouldn't you agree? He would also know where his master was most likely to run to.' The Doctor laid the standard on the table and Grey rose, placed the pistol on his side of the table, and came around to the Doctor's side to examine it. 'It's the Prince's standard, all right. Which prisoner carried this?'

'That must remain my secret for the time being,' said the Doctor.

Grey looked up sharply. 'There are ways to force your tongue.'

The Doctor smiled and shrugged. 'Why employ them, since we are both on the same side. The £30,000 reward for Prince Charles is surely enough to satisfy both of us.'

Grey came around to confront the Doctor, his eyes searching the Doctor's face. 'You have some fresh information on his whereabouts?'

The Doctor nodded and leaned forward confidentially. 'I am on the track of some,' he said, 'but . . . I need a free hand.' As Grey leaned forward to hear the Doctor's muttered confidence, the Doctor yanked the standard from the table over Grey's head, snatched up the pistol and started forward. 'Please don't call out,' said the Doctor, 'I'm not very expert with these things, you know. I'd hate it to go off in your face.' The Doctor turned Grey around and tied him up with the Prince's standard, then took the handkerchief out of his pocket as he pushed him back into his chair. The solicitor opened his mouth to speak and the Doctor immediately looked at his throat. 'Open your mouth wide,' he said. 'Good heavens, it's swollen.' As Grey automatically opened his mouth, the Doctor stuffed Grey's lace handkerchief in it, effectively gagging him. 'Well,' he said, 'that's better. I've never seen a silent lawyer before.'

There was a knock at the door. Alarmed, the Doctor looked around the room. In the corner there was a large cupboard used to store mops, brooms, and other cleaning gear. The Doctor yanked the door open, then pulled Grey over and thrust him inside. 'If you'll just wait in there,' he said, 'I think I've got another patient.' He closed and fastened the cupboard door, went back to the table and sat beside it. 'Enter,' he called.

The door opened and Perkins came in, his face the picture of astonishment as he saw the Doctor sitting there. For a moment he did not realise who the Doctor was.

'Oh, pardon,' he said, 'I thought . . .'

The Doctor leaned forward, slowly. 'You thought what?' he said.

'Uh . . .' Slightly thrown, Perkins said, 'Well, Mr Grey.' He looked around the room.

The Doctor shook his head sadly. 'Your master is a very sick man. He's gone to lie down. Lucky for him I was called in time.' As he spoke he was gradually raising himself in the chair and staring across at the short, fat Perkins who shrank back from the Doctor's intense gaze.

'Great Heavens, man,' the Doctor shouted, 'your eyes!'

Perkins jumped. 'What?'

'Your eyes. Come over here to the light. Bend back, here, that's right.' The Doctor strode around the table, pushed Perkins back over the table and, bringing out a magnifying glass from his capacious pockets, began to examine his eyes. 'Oh, I thought so, I thought so,' he said. He seized Perkins' hair and banged his head back against the table. 'How does that feel?'

'Ow!' Perkins exclaimed.

'You suffer from headaches, don't you?' He banged his head again. 'Don't answer,' said the Doctor, 'I can see it in your eyes. Here . . .' Perkins raised his hand and tried to get up. 'Do you call me a liar, sir?' said the Doctor fiercely.

'N-n-no . . . no,' said Perkins. 'No. My head does ache.'

Abruptly the Doctor got up. 'Of course,' he said, 'what do you expect when somebody bangs it on the table.' He got up and Perkins, unsupported, slid down onto the floor, his back against the table. 'It's your eyes I'm worried about, man,' said the Doctor.

Perkins looked up, alarmed. 'What did you find, Doctor?' he said. 'My eyes?'

The Doctor shrugged at the door. 'Print blindness,' he said. 'You read too much.'

Perkins was really worried now. ''Tis true,' he said, 'I am a clerk. What must I do?' He rose to his feet.

The Doctor turned back. 'If you don't wish to go blind,' he said, 'you must rest your eyes immediately for at least an hour.'

'But I'm busy,' said Perkins.

The Doctor raised his hand imperiously. 'That is my prescription. Ignore it at your peril.'

'Oh, dear me.' Perkins was really flustered now. He raised his hand to his aching head. 'I . . . It's true, I can see spots floating right in front of me.'

'Exactly,' said the Doctor.

'Now lie on that table.'

Perkins lay back on the table as the Doctor removed the little man's cravat and tied it around his eyes. 'Now, keep this around your eyes for at least an hour, to rest them. Do you understand?'

'B-but –'

'One hour. Remember. You'll hear the clock outside strike the hour. Do not get up before.' The Doctor tip-toed back towards the door leaving the clerk on the table. As he did so, a muffled thumping came from the cupboard.

63

Perkins reacted, listening, raised his head, then lowered it back again. 'What's that knocking?' he said.

'There's no knocking,' said the Doctor. 'It's in your head, in your mind, in your eyes. Just rest and the knocking'll get fainter and fainter and fainter.' The Doctor now reached the door and stealthily opened it.

'One hour, Doctor?' Perkins queried.

'One hour,' confirmed the Doctor. The Doctor blew his a kiss and then exited. As he did so, the muffled knocking from the cupboard grew louder.

9

The Doctor's New Clothes

'At last!' said Algernon. 'What took you so long, you jackanapes you?' Algernon was looking up to see the Sergeant holding a lantern over the pit. He was tired, cold and very stiff, and the belt and straps cut into his arms and legs.

'We made the best time we could, Sir,' said the Sergeant. ''Tis hard to see our way in the dark.' He spoke a little huffily. The last thing he expected to see was his officer tied and bound.

'Well don't just stand there,' said Algernon. 'Get me out of this infernal hole.'

The Sergeant turned to his men. 'Right you two. Keep watch by the Lieutenant's horse. I'll handle this.'

'Hurry up, man,' said Algernon. 'Help me out.'

The Sergeant looked down. 'It's very deep, Sir.'

Algernon said, 'Get me out at once, or I'll order you ten lashes!'

'Oh, don't mistake me, Sir,' said the Sergeant. 'I'm willing enough to try, it's just that . . .' He paused for a moment. 'We're not used to pulling officers out of pits, you see.'

'Confound you, man, what are you jabbering about?'

'What I mean to say Sir, officers don't usually fall into pits, do they?'

Algernon, understanding him, glared up. 'You'll regret this, Sergeant,' he said.

'Oh, not me, Sir,' said the Sergeant, 'it's the men I'm

thinking of. They're not used to it like. They're going to be rather curious and I wouldn't know what to tell them, would I? Curiosity makes them very dry, you see.'

Algernon groaned. The British army, like every army of that time, was run almost entirely on small bribes or threats. He realised he was in no position to offer the latter. 'All right, Sergeant, I'll see you get some money to drink with. And I hope it chokes you. I have some money in my—' He stopped, remembering what had happened to the money he carried. 'You'll get it when we return to Inverness. Now for the last time, get me out of here.'

The Sergeant started scrambling down over the edge of the pit.

Trask entered the inn room where he had left the solicitor and gazed in astonishment at Perkins, lying on the table. 'We've started shipping them—' he began. Then, 'What the blazes are you doing?'

Perkins turned his head slightly. 'I'm resting my eyes.'

'Damn your eyes,' said Trask. 'Where's your master?'

The knocking from the cupboard suddenly resumed, louder than ever.

'The Doctor said he must rest too.'

'Rest!' said Trask. He went to the cupboard, undid the catch and pulled it open, then reached in and hauled the solicitor out. 'And what have we here, then?'

Perkins sat up, took off his blindfold, and reacted in horror as Trask ripped off Grey's gag.

'A pretty sight you look, lawyer,' he laughed. 'And what may this be a cure for—St Vitus's Dance?'

'Release me,' said Grey, in a cold fury.

Trask, still laughing, started unwrapping the flag then, seeing what it was, held it up to the candlelight and examined it. Grey rubbed his arms to get the circulation back and then went over to the cowering Perkins.

'You let him escape, you idiot!' he said.

66

'I did not know. Uh . . . my head . . .'

'One more such folly,' said Grey, 'and it'll be cured forever.'

Trask turned holding up the standard. 'The Prince's standard,' he said.

Grey nodded. 'Aye, he used it to trick me. But he won't get far.' He turned to Perkins. 'Call the watch.' Then to Trask, 'And you get the next batch of prisoners aboard before they get here.'

Perkins, relieved to have got off so lightly, scurried away down the corridor, looking for the soldiers of the watch who patrolled Inverness at night. They were often to be found in the tap room of the inn. As he ran past the scullery, he didn't notice the Doctor crouched under a table laden with dirty, greasy pewter and wooden platters. At the sink there was a large, red-faced buxom woman, working a pump handle and dipping the dishes in the cold stream.

'Mollie!' The coarse rough voice echoed from the corridor. 'Where are ye? You're wanted here.'

Mollie, for that was the woman's name, turned wearily, wiping her hands on her apron. 'Bide a wee,' she called, 'I'll be there.' She turned and shuffled out of the scullery.

Once he was sure she was out of sight, the Doctor crept out from under the table and looked around him. The room was a long combined scullery and wash house. At one end there were two large wooden tubs full of soaking clothes, mostly sheets and linens. And even more interesting to the Doctor, along one wall which obviously backed onto the main fireplace of the inn because of the warmth coming through, was a long clothes-line covered with clothes of the period. To his disgust, the Doctor saw that they were all female clothes: large gowns, petticoats, aprons – some plain, some heavily embroidered. The Doctor shrugged and turned to the door, then got an idea and turned back. He looked around carefully, and then took his coat off and started taking down some of the clothes off the line.

At the far end of the corridor, Mollie, having gathered up another load of greasy platters, was slowly making her way back along the corridor to the scullery. As she came level with it, she was surprised to see a woman exit, complete in a mob-cap which almost completely covered her face, a gown, an apron, and a large cloak thrown around her shoulder. The woman was obviously quite aged and hobbled along toward the washerwoman.

'Good nicht, t' ye,' called the woman in the sing-song Inverness dialect.

Mollie shrugged her shoulders. It was a big inn and lots of people came in and out on various business, none of which was any concern of hers. All she wanted to do was get her washing done, return to her small attic room, and rest. 'Good nicht, woman,' she said wearily, and carried the platters back to the already overfilled sink. As they clattered on top of the other platters, she turned round and her eyes widened in astonishment as she saw the Doctor's coat and trousers hanging on the line.

Trask, meanwhile, was walking along the upper level of Inverness gaol, gazing down at the unfortunate prisoners beneath. The soldiers were waking them up for Trask's inspection.

'That one,' he called down, pointing at one of the prisoners, a big burly Highlander who was crouched by the door.

The sentry reached forward and pulled his shoulder, but the Highlander fell back, his eyes open, obviously dead. 'Nah, no good,' said the sentry, 'he's done for.'

'Next one then, move them along,' said Trask. He took three more steps and then looked down at the next cell.

Ben, Colin and Jamie were now standing on the top step. The water had already risen almost to their waists.

Trask pointed down. 'Those three, send them along.'

The sentry opened the door gingerly, sending the water swirling over two more steps, and Ben, Colin and Jamie gratefully followed him up from the steadily filling water dungeon. They dripped up the corridor, shivering as the cold night air hit their wet clothes.

'You'll be cold enough when you get aboard the brig,' Trask's rough voice shouted. 'Here,' he said, 'put 'em with the others.' Two of the soldiers pushed them towards a group of some fifteen dejected Highland prisoners. The British Redcoats formed ranks around them, and as Trask nodded, the Sergeant in charge ordered quick march and led them out of the gaol entrance, down the hill towards the inn.

The road was rough and flinty, and Ben was relieved to see that Colin had recovered enough to walk almost unaided. As they passed the lighted inn, heading for the cluster of tall masts that proclaimed the river, an old woman staggered out and collided with the group of prisoners. Ben nearly knocked her over.

'Sorry, old girl,' Ben apologised.

The Doctor, for it was he in his old woman's disguise, muttered something, and for a moment Ben thought he heard the familiar voice and turned sharply; but the old woman was already hobbling away through the darkness. Once out of the range of the lantern, the hunched figure paused, watched and then followed the file of soldiers as they walked along the street down towards the wharf.

They stopped before a large, half derelict warehouse and Trask led the way in. The sergeant hesitated inside and looked around suspiciously, but Trask felt in his pocket and passed the man a couple of gold coins. 'Over there,' he said.

Aided by Trask, the men cleared a couple of barrels away from the bare wooden floor to disclose a trap door with a ring bolt. As Trask nodded, they seized and pulled it open. Underneath was a set of wooden steps leading down, and the sound of water.

'Get them down there.' Trask turned to the soldiers. They started urging the tired, exhausted Highlanders down the steps towards the boat.

As Ben stumbled down the steps, he became aware of a long boat waiting to take the prisoners, manned by half a dozen rough-looking seafarers. He stopped and turned back to Trask. 'Here,' he said, 'where are you taking us?'

'Hold your tongue,' said Trask, 'you'll find out soon enough.'

'You've no mind to drown us, have you?' said Jamie.

'I wouldn't pollute the firth with you,' replied Trask. 'Now get in the boat.' They followed the others into the boat and sat on one of the thwarts.

Ben turned to Jamie as the boat pulled away. 'Quick,' he said, 'we can swim for it.' Jamie didn't answer. 'Well?' Ben demanded.

Jamie shook his head. 'I canna swim,' he admitted.

'Oh cripes!' Ben turned away disgusted.

In the shadows at the back of the warehouse, the Doctor watched the soldiers form fours and march out, then quickly made his way along to the still-open hatch and gazed down. As he looked he saw the end of the boat making its way across the dark waters of the firth towards a black, sinister-looking brig.

The long boat had now moved alongside the sheer black hulk of the brig. 'Belay there!' Trask's hoarse voice broke across the water, and the sailors rested on their oars. Above them in the moonlight – the fog now had cleared completely – they could make out a small knot of men standing at an open space between the gunwales of the brig. In their midst was the bound figure of a man. As they watched, the crew of the brig pushed the man over the side. He fell straight as an arrow, hardly making a splash in the dark waters of the firth.

As Ben and Jamie watched horrified for his return to

the surface, all they could see was an explosion of bubbles.

Trask turned round to the huddled prisoners. 'There,' he said, 'in case you think of escaping, my fine gentlemen, watch them bubbles! Once aboard the *Annabelle*, that's the only way ye'll get off it. Straight downwards. Now climb aboard.'

With the sailors standing by with drawn cutlasses, the tired Highlanders climbed up the boat ladder and onto the deck.

10

Aboard the *Annabelle*

The destination of the Scots' Highland prisoners was the ship's hold. It had obviously been used for the slave trade at some time. There were benches, rusty shackles, and four small portholes, not large enough to get more than a hand and an arm through along each side. There were already some thirty men huddled on the benches, trying to sleep, when the hatch door at the top of the companionway opened, sending a shaft of light down a rough ladder, and the latest contingent of prisoners were shoved unceremoniously down to join their comrades in the already overcrowded hold.

Ben was one of the last. He peered down and saw that there was barely room for anyone to sit, never mind lie down. 'Hey,' he said, 'there's no room for anybody down here.'

'Room enough for rebels,' the big voice of Trask bellowed after him. 'Get stowed below there.'

The three new arrivals finally made space near one of the portholes after some grumbling from the men who were first there.

'How are ye?' Jamie asked the Laird.

Colin, his eyes brighter than they had been, nodded at him. 'Thank you, Jamie, a mickle bit better, I fancy. My fever's nearly gone.'

Ben shook the man nearest him on the bench. 'Hey, mate – got any ideas where they're sending us?'

The man, a tough thick-set Scot in rough seaman's

canvas trousers and shirt, turned at at the sound of Ben's English voice and moved away from him as though stung. 'Beware of spies!' he called out in a loud voice.

There was a chorus from the other prisoners who began to wake up and look around them. 'There maen be an Englishman amongst us, Willy.' The man spoken to, Willy MacKay, struggled to his feet: a rugged man with strong features and bright blue eyes, in his early forties. 'We can strike one more blow for Scotland, lads, one more piece of vermin to stamp on.'

Ben backed away to the bulkhead, a circle of fierce Highland faces around him. 'Once down, put your boots on him. Tramp his English bones to the deck. And remember, lads,' Willy called, 'the first blow is mine.' There was a moment's silence as MacKay raised his huge gnarled fist, then a clear voice rang out over the assembled men.

'Will MacKay would ne'er strike a friend of the Prince.'

MacKay fell back. 'What? Whose voice is that?'

Colin McLaren raised himself to his feet a little shakily, aided by Jamie. 'You havena been so long away ye kenna recognise me?'

''Tis,' Willy looked closely at the Laird, 'Colin McLaren himself.' He clasped Colin's hand warmly.

Colin nodded. The men around began to relax.

'And Jamie,' said Colin. 'The son of Donald McCrimmon, a piper like his father and his father's father.'

'Aye, with no pipe,' said Jamie a little sadly.

Willy nodded to Jamie and then turned to Ben. 'And this Englishman is a friend of the Prince?'

'He's aye a friend of mine,' said Colin. 'He helped bring me here, weak but alive.'

'Then I humbly crave your pardon, sir,' said Willy. 'A friend of the McLarens is a friend of mine.'

There was a murmur of agreement from the Highlanders who now began to sink back to their former resting-places.

Ben nodded, the sweat still standing out on his brow. It had been a tight moment for him. 'Thanks, mate,' he said. He took Willy's hand and shook it. 'I'm glad to hear it.'

'How come you're here?' asked Willy.

'He's a deserter from the English Fleet,' Jamie replied.

'Aye, I'm a man of the sea myself, the master of this very vessel.'

'Hey,' said Ben, 'if you're the skipper here, what's that Trask geezer doing on the bridge?'

'That shark,' said Willy, 'was my mate. I was running arms for the Prince past the blockade, you see. Trask betrayed me and the Navy boarded the *Annabelle*. Now he runs it for King George.'

'Oh yeah?' Ben sounded sceptical, and Willy's temper flared up at his tone.

'You doubt my word?' said Willy.

'No,' said Ben hastily, 'no, skipper, not that. I just doubt that bit about him working for King George.'

'What do you mean, man?'

'We're not exactly being held like prisoners of war, are we? Hasn't it occurred to you that Trask may be using this ship without the knowledge of his King and Sovereign in some big fiddle on his own account?'

'Fiddle?' Willy was puzzled.

'Look,' said Ben, 'he'll sell us like the stinking fish he thinks we are. Slave labour, that's what we're gonna be. I think he plans to sell us over in the plantations.' There was a small chorus of dismay from the Highlanders at this. 'We'll see,' said Ben. 'It's a long way across the Atlantic.'

Polly was waiting anxiously for Kirsty to return. She was in a large barn on the outskirts of Inverness. There was a noise outside the barn door and Polly ran to it and put her eye to a crack. Outside, a man leading a small donkey laden down with pots and pans – obviously a Highland tinker – made his way along the narrow cobbled streets. Polly went back to the straw and picked up Kirsty's dirk which she had left on her plaid. Polly practised stabbing with it, but the thought of having to use a weapon was far too distasteful to her and she dropped it again.

There was a sound behind her and she turned just as Kirsty entered. 'Oh,' cried Polly, 'you did give me a fright.'

She ran forward. Kirsty was loaded down with clothes and a small sack. 'Phew,' she said, 'I'm no used to fetching and carrying. We had our servants at hame.'

'That's quite obvious,' remarked Polly drily. 'Have you got everything?'

Kirsty nodded. 'Aye, clothes for ye.' She indicated the clothes. 'Trays.' She dropped the wooden trays from the sack. 'And,' a little reluctantly, 'these oranges. Though why ye have to spend that money on oranges . . . they're no cheap you know, not up here.'

'You'll see,' said Polly. She held up the clothes. 'Oh, that's the gear. You know,' she said, forgetting whom she was talking to, 'last time I went back to the past I had to wear boys' clothes all the time.'

Kirsty stared at her blankly. 'Sometimes I canna understand a word you say.'

'Never mind,' said Polly hastily. She started drawing on the clothes over her mini-skirt and T-shirt. Finally, after settling the skirt and the petticoat and the handkerchief around her neck, copying the way that Kirsty had hers arranged, Polly was ready. 'How do I look?' she said.

Kirsty looked at her, unwilling to admit that she felt a little jealous. Polly's blonde hair and clean-cut good looks complemented the green gown she was wearing. 'Oh,' said Kirsty, 'you're bonnie enou'.'

Polly made a snub nose at her. 'Now for the oranges,' she said. Polly began emptying the oranges out on the plaid and arranging them on the two trays Kirsty had brought.

Kirsty looked with growing comprehension. 'You're not going to have us selling oranges, are ye?'

Polly suddenly reacted anxiously and turned back to Kirsty. 'Oh gosh,' she said. 'They do *have* orange sellers, don't they? I haven't got it all wrong, there is Nell Gwyn and all that?'

Kirsty looked puzzled. 'Nell Gwyn? I dinna ken her – but there are orange sellers in Scotland. Where are your eyes, Lass? But they're mostly coarse, common girls, ye ken.'

'The sort that hang around soldiers?' said Polly.

'Aye,' said Kirsty.

'Then we're orange sellers,' said Polly. Kirsty looked at her in dismay. 'How else can we find out where they've taken the Doctor and your father? There must be something we can do.'

'But if they find us out . . .'

'We still have a friend who can help us,' said Polly.

'Who?'

'Good old Algy. I wonder where he is now?'

11

At the Sea Eagle

The main dining room of the Sea Eagle was almost full with a bustling crowd of soldiers and local inhabitants eating, drinking, and occasionally starting to fight before the two massive Highland serving men came forward to eject them. In the centre there was a large fireplace with an inglenook on either side. Opposite this, there were rows of rough oak tables and benches at which most of the soldiers and townsfolk sat. On the far wall, there was a succession of wooden partitions of tables and benches affording some privacy to the occupants, who were able to pay for a complete meal instead of the hunks of bread, meat and cheese favoured by the less well-off customers at the inn.

At the far wall were two huge barrels of beer from which three soldiers were drawing large foaming mugs. Every time they drew one they made a chalk mark on the barrel, carefully watched by the proprietor of the inn who was sitting at a table near the door keeping an eye on the activities.

The Doctor, still in his old woman's disguise, shuffled up holding out a mug to be filled from the barrel. He nudged one of the soldiers who was blocking the way and said, in a cracked voice, 'Ladies first.'

The soldiers turned round and laughed at the strange-looking old woman. They started to shove her from one to the other. The Doctor put up with it for a couple of minutes, trying to preserve his disguise, and then he suddenly reached his hands out, grabbed the startled soldiers by their cross belts, and banged their heads together with the most unladylike strength. As they subsided to sitting positions on the floor, half stunned, the Doctor took the full mug from the third soldier who just stared at him and, with huffy dignity, stepped over their legs to the shelter of one of the partitions.

The attention of the soldiers was diverted from the surprisingly strong old crone when Algernon Ffinch, limping slightly, entered the room. The men from the nearest table stood to attention.

Algernon turned to them. 'Sit down, sit down!' he said.

The proprietor nodded to one of the serving wenches who hurried forward with one of the better bottles of French wine that the inn afforded. Algernon slumped into an empty booth and as a glass of wine was poured out, took it from the girl. 'Be off with you,' he said, 'I'll pay later.' He took a long draught of the wine and sank back, closing his eyes contentedly. That's better, he said to himself, much better.

The door swung open. 'In there, both of you!'

Polly and Kirsty, both in their orange-sellers' outfits, and holding their trays of oranges before them, walked into the room followed by the Sergeant, who grabbed each by the arm. The Sergeant was the same one who had pursued the girls on the moor. 'Come over and see the officer, both of you,' he said.

As they made their way across the room, the Doctor looked up from his beer and recognised them. He looked down again immediately in case they saw him and gave away his presence.

The Sergeant pushed the girls before him through the room amidst the murmurs and comments of the troops and townsfolk to Algernon's booth.

Algernon opened his eyes wearily. 'Oh, Sergeant,' he said in a bored voice, 'w-w-what is it now?'

'Take your hands off me,' snapped Kirsty.

'Kirsty, be quiet,' said Polly.

Kirsty shook her head. 'I'm not going to have a great ignorant Englishman laying hands on me.'

The Sergeant gave Polly and Kirsty a final shove, then saluted Algernon.

Polly saw Algernon and clapped her hands in pleasure, almost upsetting the orange tray around her neck in the process. 'Algernon,' she cried, 'Algernon.'

Algernon looked up in dawning horror. 'What . . . what?'

'These two look like the rebels we was hunting yesterday, Sir,' said the Sergeant.

Polly sat down in the seat beside Algernon and rested her head against his shoulder. 'Tell the nasty man we're not those rebels, Algy dear.'

Algernon drew back. 'Now just a moment,' he said.

Kirsty swung herself into the seat opposite. 'Aye,' she said, 'we're old friends, aren't we, Lieutenant!'

The Sergeant glanced from one to the other. He knew the Lieutenant's ways with women and these obviously were very familiar with him. 'I can see that,' he said.

Algernon looked up. 'That's all, Sergeant,' he said, 'go about your business.'

Some of the men standing close by began to laugh, much to Algernon's discomfiture, but the Sergeant turned and withered them with a glance. 'Right,' he said, 'time you men were back in barracks. Do you think the King pays you to idle here all night? Come on, come on . . . the last man out gets three lashes.'

The soldiers yawned, protesting, and rose to their feet as the Sergeant almost pushed them out of the room.

Once the soldiers had gone, the room was a lot quieter. The Doctor shifted from the bench he was sitting at over to the booth next to the Lieutenant and the two girls, and leaned forward to hear better.

79

Algernon looked from one to the other. 'This is really t-t-too much,' he said.

Polly pouted. 'Oh, Algy,' she said, 'we thought you might have been flattered. We turned to you for help immediately we were in trouble, didn't we Kirsty?'

Kirsty had now picked up something of the easy banter of the London girl. 'Aye,' she said, 'just the kind of person two defenceless girls would turn to in trouble.'

'I can have you thrown in prison,' threatened Algernon, trying to be fierce.

Polly looked up at the ceiling, quoting from his identity disc. 'Lieutenant Algernon Thomas Alfred Ffinch of the –'

'Stop! Stop!' Algernon looked around, and the Doctor withdrew back into his partition to keep out of sight. 'What more do you want of me,' he said, feeling very sorry for himself. 'You've got my money. I haven't even got the price of a glass of wine on me.'

Polly's voice and manner changed. 'I don't suppose the Doctor and the others have water to drink, never mind wine. Now, where are the prisoners?' she said, in a hard, business-like tone of voice.

Algernon shrugged his shoulders unhappily. 'How should I know? In prison, I expect. Where they belong.'

Kirsty shook her head. 'They're no there, we've checked. Now where are they?'

Algernon spread his hands. 'I don't know. I just round them up. You have to ask Solicitor Grey, he's the Commissioner in charge of prisoners.'

'Where can we find him?' said Polly.

'He has a room here in the inn. Now please, can I go? It's been a very long day. I had to fight a battle this morning, and now there's you two . . .'

'Oh, poor little fellow,' said Polly sarcastically. 'Go on then.'

She got up and allowed Algernon Ffinch to ease out of the partition and straighten himself. 'But mind,' she warned, 'not a word to anyone – or you-know-what.'

Algernon nodded and started making his way to the door. As he went the Doctor rose to join Polly and Kirsty, but suddenly the door opened and in came Perkins. The Doctor abruptly sat down again, lowering his head so that his face was covered by the large mob-cap.

Algernon nodded to Perkins at the door. 'Two wenches over there,' he said, pointing over to Polly and Kirsty, 'to see the Solicitor.' He then leaned forward and added, 'Frankly, he's welcome to them.' He then went out, slamming the door behind him.

Perkins glanced over and seeing two pretty girls in the booth, smiled. Despite his years and his egg-like appearance, he fanced himself as something of a ladies' man. He waddled across the room to the girls and looked from one to the other. 'Cedric Perkins, Solicitor's Clerk, at your service, ladies. What can I do for you?' There was something over-familiar and insinuating in Perkins' voice and manner that made the two girls draw back slightly.

'Where is Mr Grey?' said Polly.

'The Commissioner,' Perkins said with dignity, 'is seeing to his duties, Miss. He's giving some rebel prisoners the choice between life and death.'

In the hold of the brig, Solicitor Grey stood by the ladder leading down to the crowded hold, some parchments in his hand. Standing beside him, Trask, more threatening than ever, was playing with a long cat-o'-nine-tails whip – a collection of knotted strips of leather bound to a wooden handle, and the most feared means of punishment at sea.

'Silence, you bilge rats,' Trask shouted. 'The Solicitor has news for ye.'

The men in the hold who had been muttering to themselves now fell silent.

'Rebels,' said Grey, 'your attention, please. I have an offer of clemency from his Gracious Majesty King George.' There was a murmur of protest at this.

'Quiet!' Trask's huge voice rang round the room again. He cracked the whip at the nearest man, who drew back clutching his arm in pain. The room quietened down again.

Grey looked reflectively around the room. 'The clemency can be withdrawn, so hark ye.'

'We're listening.' A voice came from the back of the hold, and Trask pricked his ears up as he recognised the familiar voice of Willy MacKay.

'It has pleased His Majesty,' said Grey, 'to declare that whereas there are a great many of his rebellious subjects in gaol, a speedy example must be made of them.'

'Clemency,' Colin's voice carried on from the back of the hold.

'Clemency,' Grey repeated. 'Therefore it is ordained that there will be those required as witnesses to turn King's evidence.'

'Traitors, you mean,' Jamie called out.

Grey smiled a thin cold smile that made his long narrow face even more forbidding. 'Those not wanting to turn King's evidence will be hanged immediately,' he said.

A storm of protest broke out at this. Trask waved his cat-o'-nine-tails and strode forward, and the murmurs died down.

'Wait, Mr Trask,' Grey called. Trask, who was about to start belabouring the defenceless men around him, lowered the whip. 'There is one other alternative.' Grey turned and beckoned up the ladder, and two seamen, the first carrying a small table, the second an inkstand and a pen, came down. Both men were armed with two long pistols at their belts. Grey held up the sheaf of papers. 'Plantation workers are wanted for His Majesty's colonies in the West Indies. I have here contracts for seven years. Sign your names to these and you will have free transportation to your new homes and a chance of liberty when your seven years' indentures are completed.'

His words seemed to cast a spell over the room. The men who a few minutes before had been looking forward to almost certain death now began to take in the meaning of Grey's words and their faces lightened.

'I'm offering you life and hope,' said Grey. 'Who will be the first to sign?'

One of the Highlanders stood up and walked forward to the table. Grey spread the top contract form and dipped the pen in the ink, handing it to the man. The Highlander bent down when Willy stood up abruptly at the back of the hold, his voice ringing over the assembled prisoners.

'Dinna touch that pen!' He made his way forward through the men. 'I ken fine what ye offer, Solicitor,' he said. 'I've seen these West Indies plantations. Not one of you who sign that document will live your seven years. Better a quick and honourable death at the end of King George's rope than a slow living death of constant toil, lashings and yellow fever.'

The Highlanders were now deeply split and argued furiously among themselves.

Grey turned to Trask. 'Who is that man?' he said.

Trask mouthed grimly, 'Willy MacKay, former master of this vessel.'

Grey nodded, understandingly. 'Ah, I see,' he said.

Trask's hand felt for the butt of a long horse pistol sticking out of his pocket. 'We should have disposed of him long ago.' He moved forward through the hold, but Grey grabbed him by the arm.

'No,' said Grey, 'not now. Later perhaps, Trask, later,' he whispered. He raised his hand for silence. 'Listen to me. You have heard what Master MacKay offers you: death with honour – if that's what you call it, lingering at the end of a halter. Followed by quartering, and the like courtesies reserved for His Majesty's rebels. What I offer is life, and a chance to work for your liberty.'

Willy shook his head bitterly. 'Liberty,' he scorned; but the men were beginning to disregard him, and elbow him back into the crowd.

'Make your choice,' called Grey. 'Those who wish to sign step over here.' He indicated the left side of the hold. 'And those who wish to hang or . . .' An idea struck him, a clever, legalistic idea, playing on the ingrained loyalty of the Highland men. 'Of course,' he said, 'turn King's evidence . . .' he bowed slightly to Willy MacKay '. . . over there.'

There was a moment's silence as the Highlanders looked uncertainly at one another, then began to move to the left-hand side. By a brilliant stroke, Grey had made it seem that those who would not join the men contracted to the West Indies plantations had in mind betraying their fellows and turning King's evidence against them.

Jamie moved forward and stood beside Willy, realising the implications of the situation. 'The fools!' he said.

'Stop!' cried Willy. 'Stop men!' But eventually, only Colin, Jamie, Willy and Ben were left on the right-hand side of the hold; the rest formed a long line and began making their signatures, crosses or thumbprints on the sheets of parchment.

Grey looked over and counted. 'Only four for the gallows, I think,' he said.

'Ben!' Jamie was shocked to see Ben go up to the signing table.

'What about me?' said Ben, 'can I sign?'

Grey smiled and waved his hand down at the paper.

'I can read, you know,' said Ben. 'Can I read it first?' Ben pushed into the line of men and bent over the table. The next instant he seized the three sheets of fine parchment and tore them into pieces.

Trask spun forward, swung the heavy handle of his cat-o'-nine tails, and knocked Ben unconscious onto the deck. Willy and Jamie moved forward, but the sailors beside Trask levelled their pistols at their chests and said to stand back.

For once Grey showed his anger. 'Clap him into irons,' he said. 'When I return with the new contracts, bind him and drop him from the yard-arm.' He turned and climbed out of the hold as the sailors bent down, picked up the unconscious Ben, and loaded him on their shoulders.

12

The Little Auld Lady

Perkins, meanwhile, was sitting with a flagon of sherry in front of him, facing a nervous Polly and Kirsty, and obviously enjoying playing with them as a cat plays with a mouse. In the next partition the Doctor sat listening, but unable to act.

Polly started to get up. 'Mr Grey doesn't seem to be coming, does he?' she said. 'I think we'd better be off.'

Perkins leaned across and restrained her from going. 'My dear young lady,' he said, 'surely you won't deprive an old fellow of your charming company? I assure you he won't be long.'

'Nevertheless,' said Polly, 'I think that –'

'I insist.' Perkins' tone dropped its usually oily smoothness and became firm.

'No,' said Polly, pushing his hand away.

'Then,' said Perkins, 'I shall rouse the watch. They may be interested in two such genteel orange wenches.'

Polly stared helplessly at him for a moment and then sat down again.

'That's better,' he said. 'Now to pass the time. What say you to a round of whist?'

Polly looked at him. 'Whist?' she said. 'I can't play whist.'

Perkins felt in his pocket and brought out a pack of playing cards and placed them on the table. 'It's quite easy,' he said, 'you can soon learn.' He started to deal the cards just as an old woman came around the side of the partition and slid in next to him, speaking in a quavery voice.

'You need four for whist.'

Perkins hardly bothered to look at the bundle of clothes that had thrust itself in next to him. 'Kindly remove yourself, madam.'

Polly looked closely across the table at the face beneath the cap and, recognising it, clapped her hand over her mouth to stifle her giggles. The Doctor, in no hurry, spread his skirts and picked up and finished off Perkins' glass of sherry.

'Nothing finer than a round of whist,' squeaked the Doctor. 'Who is to deal?'

Perkins, his fat jowls quivering indignantly, stood up to his full five foot four. 'Madam, I told you –' he raised his hand to call for the innkeeper, then became aware of Grey's pistol levelled at his heart.

'I'm sure you'd oblige an auld woman,' the Doctor said in his piping Scots' tone.

Perkins hand fell, his mouth gaped open. He looked closely at the Doctor's face. 'The German Doctor!' he exclaimed.

The Doctor nodded. 'Yes,' he said. 'Uh, would you deal, Kirsty, and perhaps,' he added 'you would like to count the trumps, Perkins?'

Perkins slowly subsided, feeling the pressure of the Doctor's pistol against his ribs. Kirsty expertly cut the cards and started dealing. Across the room, the door flung open and Grey entered in a furious temper. The Doctor saw him, lowered his head so that his face was obscured by his bonnet and, hiding the gun with his shawl, managed to keep the muzzle pointed at Perkins' waistcoat. 'Don't say a word,' he whispered.

Grey looked around the room, then spotted Perkins at the table and strode over. 'Perkins!' he said, 'what the devil are you doing, man?'

Perkins opened his mouth to speak and felt the nudge

of the pistol barrel. 'Ah,' he said, 'I'm just playing a round of cards, Mr Grey.'

Grey gave the others a quick glance. 'Indeed,' he said, 'well, you can just come up to my room with me, we need more contracts.' He turned away.

'Mr Grey . . .' Polly began.

The Doctor leaned across and touched Polly on the arm, shaking his head.

'Oh, nothing . . .' said Polly.

Grey looked keenly back, struck by the, as he would have put it, aristocratic English accent, but there were more important matters to see to. He turned on his heel and walked out. 'Hurry up, Perkins,' he shouted over his shoulder.

Perkins rose. 'I must go,' he said.

The Doctor stopped him for a moment. 'Remember you've seen nothing,' he said.

'Eh?' Perkins replied.

'Your eyes, remember,' said the Doctor. 'You wouldn't want another headache, now, would you?'

'N-n-no, of course not,' said Perkins.

'I'll tell you what's going to happen,' said the Doctor, 'we ladies are going to leave first. You're going to sit here comfortably for ten minutes before you get up to go.'

Perkins stared at him in a complete panic. 'But Mr Grey –' he began.

The Doctor continued: 'Because I shall be watching you for all that time, and one move, and . . .' He raised the pistol again.

Perkins nodded his head unhappily, sweat pouring off his brow. 'Yes, sir, I understand sir.'

'Come girls,' said the Doctor, 'let us leave this rough place. I'm sure he'd have cheated anyway.' As they walked across to the door he looked back at Perkins. 'Ten minutes, remember.'

Perkins nodded, almost in tears. 'Ten minutes.'

Once outside the inn, Polly and Kirsty looked around quickly, then urged the Doctor forward.

'Where are we going?' said the Doctor.

'Don't worry,' said Polly, 'we've found a hiding place. It's quite safe. Come on.'

Following the back lanes of Inverness, they came to the barn set at the back of a large stables.

'We're quite safe in here,' said Polly, opening the door. Once inside, the three, out of breath, sank down in the hay, and Polly began laughing. 'The sight of that horrid little man's face,' she said, 'when you stuck the gun under his nose.'

For the first time, Kirsty also started laughing. 'It was a picture right enou'.'

The Doctor brought out the pistol, aimed it at the far side of the bar, cocked it, and started to squeeze the trigger.

'Careful, Doctor!' said Polly, alarmed.

'Och,' said Kirsty, 'you'll bring the town down upon us.'

The Doctor pressed the trigger, the lock snapped harmlessly forward. He lowered the gun. 'Quite safe,' said the Doctor, 'I unloaded it last night. Nasty dangerous things, guns,' he added, and put it back in his pocket.

Polly couldn't help giggling again. The relief of being back with the Doctor after the desperate hours of having to be the leader and make the decisions made her feel quite light-headed. 'You know that gear rather suits you, Doctor,' she said.

The Doctor looked down at it, interested in spite of himself. 'Do you really think so?' he said. He looked over at Kirsty.

'You're the very image of my auld granny McLaren,' she said. 'Only she canna speak a word of English.'

'You're marvellous, Doctor,' said Polly. 'You've even managed to cheer Kirsty up.'

Kirsty's mouth turned down again as she remembered her situation. 'Aye, I'd forgotten where we were,' she said.

Polly turned to the Doctor. 'What're we going to do, Doctor?'

The Doctor flung himself back on the hay and closed his eyes. 'Oh, it's so comfortable here,' he said. 'What do you suggest we should do?'

Polly wailed despairingly. 'Oh Doctor, don't start that again. Don't go sleepy on us now, we've got to do something.'

The Doctor closed his eyes. 'Go ahead.'

'Oh.' Polly's relief at having shifted the responsibility onto the Doctor evaporated quickly. 'Well,' she said, 'if we only knew where the others were . . .'

The Doctor's voice came drowsily across. 'On the brig *Annabelle* out in the firth,' he said.

'What?' said Kirsty.

'A ship. The master's name is Trask.' He opened his eyes and shook his head. 'Not a nice man, you wouldn't like him.' He closed his eyes again.

'Doctor!' Polly flung herself on her knees beside him and dug him in the ribs. 'Keep awake! If they're on the ship we've got to get them off it.'

'Orrr?' said the Doctor sleepily.

'Or,' said Polly. She had her hand to her head, thinking hard. 'We try and capture the ship.'

'What would we do that for?' said Kirsty.

Polly said, 'Well surely you could sail to somewhere safe with it. Wasn't France your ally, or something?'

The Scots girl set her lips and shook her head slowly. 'I'll no leave Scotland for anything,' she said.

'It would be safer,' said the Doctor.

'Never!' said Kirsty.

The Doctor sat up suddenly. 'It wouldn't have to be for long, you know. Just for . . . let's see . . .' With his encyclopaedic memory for dates and times, the Doctor ran his mind back through the history of the Jacobite rebellion. How long before there would be a general amnesty and pardon and they could return to their glens? 'Let's see, it would be . . .' then he stopped himself. 'No,' he said, 'not very long, just a while.'

Poor Kirsty had enough on her mind without wondering how a man could see into the future in this way.

'Just for a while, and then it will be safe to return here again.'

Kirsty still shook her head obstinately. 'Why should I leave my ain country?' she said.

The Doctor lay back again. 'Please yourself,' he said, 'but you and your father may both lose your lives if you stay in the glen.'

'Well,' said Kirsty, reluctantly, 'if you're sure there's no other way.'

Polly was also remembering her history a little, but she wasn't as clear about it as the Doctor. 'The Doctor says it won't be for long,' she said.

'What must we do then?' said Kirsty.

'We must make a plan.' She looked at the Doctor. 'Doctor, I know you've got a plan for us. It's just like you. Come on, what is it?'

'No,' said the Doctor, closing his eyes again.

'Oh, come on, I know you better than that. You must have a plan.'

The Doctor still shook his head. 'Not really,' he said.

The two girls looked at him in despair and he opened one eye. 'But I have got a wee idea,' he said.

Polly sat back, relieved. Just the Doctor playing one of his tricks as usual. She looked reproachfully at him. 'Oh Doctor!' she said.

As though recharged and filled with fresh energy, the Doctor sprang onto his knees. 'Just thought of it,' he said. 'Won't work, of course.' And then as their faces fell again, he said, 'but it's worth a try. Anybody got any money?'

Polly nodded. 'We've seventeen guineas left. We took it from the English Lieutenant.'

'Ah,' the Doctor rubbed his hands, 'a fortune in these days. Now, we need weapons, lots of them . . . and a rowing boat.'

'I can get the boat,' said Kirsty. 'I've a cousin McLaren who runs a fishing smack out of Inverness.'

The Doctor nodded. 'Good, and the weapons can be bought from the English soldiers. They must have hoards of Rebel weapons as souvenirs by now.'

'But will they sell them to us?' said Polly.

The Doctor nodded. 'You don't know the English soldier. He'd sell you his mother for sixpence.'

'And then?' said Kirsty.

'We smuggle them out to the brig,' said the Doctor.

Polly nodded her head excitedly. 'Yes Doctor, then?'

'And then,' the Doctor's face became blank, 'I dunno.' He yawned. 'I expect we'll find something to do once we get there. I must sleep now.' The Doctor fell back in the hay, closed his eyes, and with the particular gift he had was instantly fast asleep.

'Oh no,' Polly leaned over and tried to wake the Doctor. She looked at Kirsty who was also examining the Doctor.

'Och, he's fast asleep,' said Kirsty. The two girls looked at each other over the sleeping Doctor.

'I'm scared to fall asleep,' said Kirsty, 'in case I dinna wake up in time.'

'Oh, don't worry,' said Polly, 'the Doctor will wake us up in an hour. He's like that. Must have an inbuilt alarm clock.' The two girls snuggled down in the hay beside the sleeping Doctor.

13

A Ducking For Ben

Across the chill, mist-shrouded waters of the firth a bell was tolling midnight. Grey, wrapped up in his cloak, and Perkins were being rowed across to the brig. As Grey clambered on deck, followed by Perkins clutching a battered portfolio, Trask leaned down and helped them aboard.

'Mr Trask,' said Grey.

'Aye,' said Trask.

'Is everything in readiness?'

'It is.'

'If anyone tries the same trick,' said Grey, 'shoot him down immediately, Captain, do you understand?'

'I'll quarter him on the spot, don't worry about that,' said Trask.

'I've had Perkins copy out three new contracts, just to make sure. We'll need two of them signed and sealed tonight.'

Trask's face set, his brows coming down, his face jutting out, so that Perkins, almost involuntarily, moved a pace backwards. 'Every man jack of them will sign. If not with ink, then with blood,' said Trask. ''Tis all one to me.'

Grey, making his way along towards the companion-way down to the hold, turned. 'No,' he said, 'you're not dealing with slaves, man. These Highlanders have high courage and resolution. If you flog but one of them they'll stand together and refuse to sign a thing. You'll undo all I've worked for. When they're safely sold in Barbados, they can be whipped to death for all I care – until then use a light fist, or you'll answer to me.'

Unused to being taken to task in this way – and on his own quarterdeck – Trask bristled for a moment, then shrugged his shoulders. 'And the London deserter, what am I to do with him?'

'Proceed with the ducking,' Grey rejoined. 'He will be a useful example to the rest. Perkins, go below and commence signing the contracts.'

Perkins nodded and hurried away to the companionway leading below.

Grey turned back to Trask. 'Bring the deserter on deck.'

Meanwhile in the barn, Polly and Kirsty were sitting waiting for the Doctor. Both girls were very tired and yawning. In front of them on Kirsty's plaid were a broken sword, a pitchfork, and a couple of rusty kitchen knives. Kirsty yawned. 'We could have stayed asleep for all the good we've done,' she said.

'You're right,' Polly groaned. 'It's all right for the Doctor. Give him an hour and he packs a night's sleep in. He's fresh again.' She looked down at the meagre collection of weapons. 'We didn't do very well, did we?'

Kirsty shook her head. 'They wouldna take me seriously.'

Polly nodded. 'Nor me. I hope the Doctor's had better luck than this.'

There was a soft knock at the barn door. The girls rushed over. 'Who's there?' called Polly.

'Me,' the Doctor's voice came softly through a crack in the door. They pulled it open, and the Doctor entered trundling a small hand barrow covered with a piece of tarpaulin. They closed the door behind them and turned back.

'What have you got there, Doctor?' asked Polly excitedly. 'Let's see?'

The Doctor shook his head. 'No, let's see what you've got, first.'

Polly sighed. 'Don't tease us,' she said. 'Look.' She led him over and the two girls showed him their meagre supply of weapons.

The Doctor nodded encouragingly. 'Well, it's a start.' He went back to the barrow and whipped off the tarpaulin with the air of a conjurer performing a trick. The barrow was loaded to the brim with swords, muskets, dirks, and pistols.

Kirsty gave a small scream. 'Whee!' she said. 'You must've robbed the Duke's arsenal.'

The Doctor shrugged modestly. 'Something like that,' he said.

'That's super, Doctor,' said Polly.

Kirsty leaned over to pick up a heavily ornamented pistol. 'Here's a bonnie one,' she said.

The Doctor looked at her hand holding the pistol and then leaned over and grabbed her wrist. 'One moment,' he said.

'What is it?' said Kirsty, scared.

'Your ring.' Kirsty tried to cover it.

'Show me.'

'Oh that,' Polly said, 'it's her father's. She won't let you touch it. Or even mention it.'

But the Doctor firmly took Kirsty's hand and she reluctantly let him see the ring.

'I see why,' he said, looking her in the eye.

'What's the secret?' said Polly.

'It's not her father's ring,' said the Doctor.

'You lie.'

'Then why has it got the Stuart seal on it?' said the Doctor.

'My father bade me not to tell where he got it.'

'Until the right time,' countered the Doctor, 'and that time has now arrived, Kirsty.'

There was a moment's hesitation. The girl looked

down at the ring, obviously struggling with her feelings, and then said, 'The Prince gave it to my father off his own finger in the heat of battle.' She raised her head proudly. 'He saved the Prince's life, ye ken.'

'Then it is right and proper that it should now save *his* life.' He held out his hand. 'May I have it, please?'

Kirsty looked at him for a moment and then, showing her newfound trust in this strange man who had come from . . . where? . . . Somewhere beyond Kirsty's limited experience, she slowly pulled the ring off her finger and gave it to him.

The Doctor studied it carefully. 'Ah,' he said, 'I wonder.' And then, snapping his fingers, he said, 'Of course, bait!'

'Pardon, Doctor?' said Polly.

The Doctor winked at her. 'Bait. For a very greedy man.' He tried the ring on his finger, and then held his hand up, admiring it. He turned to the girls. 'Now,' he said, 'we have to think about how to get this lot'—he indicated the barrow of weapons—'to the quayside undetected.'

Ben, his arms and legs bound, was standing on deck as a sailor adjusted a rope around his waist. The rope was suspended from one of the booms, which protruded over the side of the ship. At a signal from Trask, Ben was hauled six foot in the air and then, as the sailors worked the pulleys, the boom swung out over the dark waters of the firth. Trask looked over at Grey, who nodded, and at Trask's signal, the sailors released the rope. Ben plummeted down with a splash into the dark, cold waters. The watching men waited for the signal from Trask to bring the young sailor back to the surface, but Trask, his arm upraised, waited. The seconds ticked by. Finally, Grey, who saw the loss of the several hundred pounds that Ben would fetch in the labour markets of the West Indies, nodded impatiently to Trask, and Trask dropped his hand. The men hauled, and then fell over backwards on the deck, as the rope snaked up – with no Ben on the end!

'What on earth!' Grey stepped forward and stared at the water, but there was no sign of the young Cockney. They waited for the tell-tale bubbles, but again nothing broke the surface.

Finally Trask shrugged his shoulders. 'Good riddance,' he said. 'It'll be a warning to the rest.'

Grey shrugged his shoulders. 'Perkins should have finished getting the contracts signed,' he said. He turned away, heading for the companionway to the hold, followed by Trask.

If their eyes could have penetrated the dark, murky sea water, they would have seen Ben swimming strongly towards the shore. He had managed to get out of his bonds by an old trick, often practised by sailors in the Royal Navy. Now, his lungs bursting, he came up for air behind a moored rowing boat, a safe distance away from the brig. When his tortured lungs had finally had their fill of air, he turned and, despite the chilling cold, set out with a long, steady overarm stroke for the shore.

Luckily Ben was a very strong swimmer, and during the icy half-mile stretch was able to vary his stroke: first the crawl, then the breast stroke, the back stroke to give him a much-needed respite, and then a stroke his father had taught him, that was rarely used or taught at the London baths where Ben had learned his swimming – the side stroke.

Finally, chilled almost to the marrow, Ben grasped the rungs of a ladder protruding from the closest Inverness wharf to the brig, and hauled himself up, flopping on the wooden boards like a stranded whale gasping for breath, his eyes closed. Something moved close to his face. He opened his eyes and saw before him the white gaiters of an English sentry, and the butt of a musket.

Ben shook his head wearily. 'Oh no, not after all that!

Okay,' he said. He rolled over on his back. 'I give up.'

A familiar voice said, 'You give up awfully easily for an intrepid British tar!'

'What?!' Ben, fatigue forgotten, sat up abruptly and stared at the sentry. Under the tall grenadier's hat there was a familiar face. 'Doctor!' he called.

'Well, of course,' said the Doctor, 'who else would be walking around a jetty at one in the morning, dressed as an English sentry?'

Ben shivered and got to his feet. 'You've got a point there. But why?'

'Why not,' said the Doctor, 'I like it here. And besides, it keeps the other soldiers away.'

Ben nodded as the Doctor took his heavy greatcoat off and wrapped it around the young soldier's shoulders. 'Of course. Have you got somewhere warm to go to after guard duty? I'm frozen,' he said.

The Doctor nodded. 'Just the place. I think we can supply some warm clothes and food to go with them.'

Ben closed his eyes in ecstasy. 'Food,' he said, 'my stomach's forgotten the meaning of that word.'

The Doctor said, 'Just let me return this musket to the boat and I'll be right with you.'

Ben shook his head, puzzled. 'The boat?'

'Yes,' said the Doctor. 'It's loaded with a few wee gifties for our friends aboard the *Annabelle*.' As Ben watched, the Doctor walked over and, leaning down, peeled back the tarpaulin from a rowing boat tied alongside the wharf. Inside, the moonlight caught the sharp glint of the swords and bayonets.

14

Where is the Prince?

Inside the cabin of the brig, a small, rather cramped room with an overhead skylight, a long table firmly screwed down to the deck and two long benches likewise fastened, Grey, Perkins and Trask were examining the signed indentures which were spread out on the table. Trask, at the far end of the table, was noisily gurgling down the remnants of a bottle of wine.

'There, sir,' said Perkins, 'duly signed and attested; it just wants your signature.'

Grey nodded a little grimly. 'Not before time,' he said. He dipped a quill pen in the ink pot that Perkins brought out of his invariable leather portfolio, and started signing the documents.

Trask rose to his feet a little unsteadily, turned, opened a cupboard set in the side wall, and from a well-filled wine rack carefully selected another bottle of red Burgundy. He turned back and waved it in front of Grey. 'A little wine for your cold heart, lawyer?'

Grey looked up, an expression of distaste on his long face. 'I never mix strong liquors and business. I would advise you to do the same, Mr Trask. You sail with the morning tide, if you remember.'

Trask sat down again and poured himself some wine. 'Happen it's too foggy to sail,' he said expansively. 'What then?'

Grey leaned forward, his eyes piercing. 'You sail, Mr Trask,' he said, 'fog or no fog.'

'Aye, and crash' – he slapped the table – 'this old girl's timbers on Chanonry Point.'

Grey leaned back, his tone heavy with sarcasm. 'I took you for a seaman.'

Trask gave him a lopsided smile, revealing a row of blackened, broken teeth. 'Why that I am, good sir. Trask will get your cargo of little beauties to Barbados, never fear.' Then, suddenly irritated by the lawyer's contemptuous manner, he pointed a stubby finger across the table. 'That's what really counts, lawyer, not those dried up bits of parchment of yours.'

'Without these bits of parchment,' said Grey, 'we'd all be sailing afoul of the King's law.'

'Law? Huh,' Trask gave a hoarse laugh. 'What does the law, or anyone, care for these Highland cattle we carry?'

Grey raised his eyebrows. 'Nothing,' he said. 'But to take these cattle fresh to the slave plantations – before their health has been sapped by His Majesty's prisons – that takes skill and preparation.'

'And what would happen to you if this trade were to be discovered by the Duke?' Trask's dark face had grown sly, his eyes glinting across the table under their bushy black brows.

Grey paused, felt in his pockets for his snuff box, and before answering opened it, placed a little on his thumb and took a delicate sniff. 'It will never happen, Trask. There are only three of us privy to the secret. I can answer for myself and for Perkins, eh?' He turned to Perkins quickly.

Perkins nodded hastily. 'Oh yes, yes sir, indeed you may answer for me.'

Then Grey turned back. 'You, Captain, must answer for yourself.'

Again Trask saw that he had pushed this calm, unsmiling man opposite too far. He shrugged his shoulders, trying to bluff his way out of the situation.

'All but in jest. You know me, Solicitor, I'm your man.'

Grey nodded. 'Aye,' he said. He took another pinch of snuff. 'And you'll remain so, Mr Trask.'

Inside the barn, the four fugitives had just finished a meal of stew, bread, tea and cold beef.

Ben was dressed, a little self-consciously, in knee breeches, ruffled shirt, waistcoat, and the long embroidered jacket of the period.

'Cor,' he said, 'that's better. Never thought I'd live to see a meal like that again.'

Polly turned to him, a little puzzled. 'How did you manage to get loose?' she asked. 'Underwater, too?'

Ben inflated his chest a little. He always enjoyed showing off for Polly; the opportunity for it came all too rarely. 'The old Houdini trick, duchess. You flex your muscles when they tie you up.' He showed them by wrapping a piece of rope around his biceps. 'Then, when you're ready, you let your muscles relax, like this.' Ben exhaled the air from his chest and let his muscles relax, and the rope fell off. 'See? You're half the size you were before. Get it?'

'Nay,' said Kirsty, puzzled.

Polly looked at him a little suspiciously. 'And that's all there is to it, Ben?'

'Almost all,' said Ben.

'Huh,' Polly sniffed. 'I bet.'

They turned as the Doctor emerged from one of the stalls, now dressed in his own clothes again. He was brushing at his coat a little anxiously, obsessed by a couple of new stains that had appeared on the already well worn sleeve.

'Oh, you got your own clothes back,' said Polly.

The Doctor nodded, indignantly. 'Can you imagine! I found them thrown out on the rubbish heap behind the inn!'

'Yeah,' said Ben drily, 'amazing, ain't it.'

Polly smiled slyly and winked at the others. 'I liked you best in your dress, Doctor.'

The Doctor turned and clapped his hands, calling them around him. 'Now,' he said, 'do we all know what we've got to do? Ben?'

Ben nodded. 'I take you out to the ship in the rowing boat, paddle around the other side and, while they're sorting you out, I hand in the weapons through the porthole.'

Polly frowned and shook her head. 'While Kirsty and I just sit here waiting for you to get back – if you ever do? Nothing doing!'

'Aye,' said Kirsty, and the Doctor noted with amusement she was picking up some of Polly's independence, 'we've done enough waiting.'

'It may be dangerous,' said the Doctor, 'they may not swallow my ploy.'

'Aye,' said Ben, 'and they may stop me in the boat, even with this on.' He pulled a large tam-o'-shanter from the clothes pile and pulled it over his head. It covered most of his face as well. The others laughed.

'There,' said Polly, 'you'll get into terrible trouble without us, eh Kirsty?'

Kirsty nodded firmly. 'Aye, terrible.'

The Doctor looked from one to the other. 'All right,' he said, giving in, 'you and Kirsty come with us in the boat.' He looked at Kirsty. 'You could be rather useful at that.'

'What do you want me to do?' said Ben.

'I've got a better idea for you,' said the Doctor.

In the hold there was one dim lantern containing a single candle, throwing out a faint light that hardly penetrated over the sleeping Highlanders to a small group at the far end by the porthole.

Colin, Willy and Jamie were still very much awake and conferring while their fellow prisoners slept.

'I canna believe it,' said Willy in disgust. 'They played right into Grey's hands. My own crew amongst them.'

'Ah, can you blame them,' said Colin. 'A poor choice – the gallows or the plantations. A man will clutch at any straw to save his neck.'

'What will they do with us?' said Jamie.

Colin sighed. 'I'm afraid they'll make an example of us. Like that poor deserter friend of yours. Once Trask gets away to sea –'

Willy broke in. 'He'll no let me live, that's aye certain. Ah wheel, better a fast death than a slow lingering one under the overseers. I've nae regrets, ye ken.'

'If I could but see my Kirsty again, I'd die content,' said Colin. He leaned back against the porthole, his eyes closing, the wound still throbbing in his shoulder.

In the cabin, Grey and Perkins were completing their final accounts in a black leather-covered ledger.

'That makes a total of three and a half thousand guineas. You'll collect it in gold on delivery of the prisoners, and render strict accounting to me,' Grey turned to Perkins. 'Is that quite clear?'

Perkins nodded, rubbing his hands. 'Yes, Mr Grey sir, very clear. You may trust me to the death, sir.'

Grey pulled out a watch from his waistcoat and looked at it. 'It's very late,' he said, 'I must return ashore. I shall expect you in London by the end of October.' He rose. 'Keep a close eye on our Mr Trask, I do not trust him.'

As he spoke, there was a sudden commotion on the deck over their heads – a stamping of feet, and Trask's rough voice calling out some commands.

The next instant, the cabin door creaked open and Trask entered, followed by two sailors holding the Doctor by the arm.

Trask turned to the solicitor. 'We've got company, Mr Grey. Caught him coming over the side – bold as a Welsh pirate.'

The Doctor bowed. 'Delighted to meet you again, Solicitor.'

Grey stared over at him, and smiled grimly. 'You may not be as delighted when we part company this time, Doctor.'

The Doctor grimaced. 'If you'll tell these good fellows to let go of my arms, I have a small token for you.'

Grey leaned back in his chair on the bench. 'I haven't forgotten the last one.' He turned to the sailors. 'All right, let him go.'

Trask, meanwhile, had been looking from one to the other, trying to make out what was going on. Now he intervened. 'Let me have him. I'll soon change his tune.'

Grey turned. 'Silence!' he said, sharply. Then, to Perkins, 'Perkins, shut the door.' He turned back to the Doctor. 'Well, go on.'

The Doctor carefully smoothed his shabby coat down and winced slightly as he rubbed his arm, now free from the rough grasp of the sailors. He then slowly patted his pockets in turn. 'Now, let's see,' he said, 'where did I put it? Uh . . . not this one' – he felt his top left-hand pocket – 'I think I transferred it to this one . . .' He felt on the right side. 'Ah, no . . . no, no, that one.' Eventually he dug deep down into his right-hand tail pocket, and with triumph brought out something in his closed fist and held it out. As his fingers extended, Grey, Perkins and Trask, who had leaned forward to see the contents of the Doctor's hand, saw – a conker. 'Here,' said the Doctor – and then looked at it in dismay. 'Oh, no . . .'

Trask leaned forward, seized the Doctor's lapels, and lifting him off his feet, held him against the bulkhead. 'Why, ye scurvy bilge rat.'

Grey, also rose, his eyes daggers. 'I suggest you find whatever you're looking for, Doctor, before I leave you to the tender mercies of Mr Trask.'

The Doctor, meanwhile, had his hand in his left-hand

tail pocket, and nodded, frightened. 'I've got it, got it,' he said.

Trask released him, and the Doctor brought out Kirsty's ring and placed it on the table.

Grey glanced down at it. 'If this is another of your humours, Doctor . . .'

'Look at the seal,' said the Doctor.

Closely watched by Perkins and Trask, Grey held the ring up under the suspended cabin lantern, then reacted in surprise. 'The Stuart arms!' he said.

'Well, Mr Grey?' said the Doctor.

'Where did you get this?'

The Doctor drew himself up proudly. 'From the hand of Prince Charles himself.'

There was a gasp from the other three men in the cabin.

'Where?' said Grey.

'In prison,' said the Doctor.

Grey shook his head. 'I don't follow you.'

'It's quite easy,' said the Doctor. 'The Prince disguised himself as a Highlander and was taken prisoner with the rest of the rebels.'

Despite himself, Grey's steely eyes gleamed as he leaned forward. 'And where is he now?'

The Doctor started twiddling his thumbs. 'I wonder what that information would be worth. Let's see now . . .' He raised his hand and started counting on his fingers.

Trask gave a sudden growl, his hand going to his cutlass, and pulled it out of his sheath. 'Leave him to me,' he said, 'I'll burn it out of him.'

'No,' Grey stopped him. 'What do you think it's worth, Doctor?' he said, his tone heavy with sarcasm.

The Doctor looked up at the deck head for a moment before replying. 'Shall we say . . .' he finished his computation, '. . . ten thousand guineas, yes?'

Meanwhile outside, Kirsty and Polly, their oars carefully muffled to avoid making a sound, had rowed across the firth and were now scraping against the side of the brig. Kirsty stood up and looked through the small porthole. She turned back to Polly and shook her head. 'Not this one,' she said, 'it must be the one further round.'

Polly, grasping the rough timbers of the brig, started pulling the boat further round towards the other porthole from which a faint light was shining.

'Right,' whispered Kirsty.

Polly leaned over the bow and grasped one of the Brig's securing lines stretched out to a nearby buoy, and held the boat alongside the hull.

Kirsty stood on one of the thwarts and gazed through the porthole. Inside, Jamie and Willy had dozed off. Colin, his wound still throbbing, was leaning back beside the porthole, in a dream between waking and sleeping. He heard a voice that seemed to come from his thoughts, which were back with his family in the beautiful glen they called home.

'Father. Father. Father,' the voice called.

Colin, still in his dreams, smiled. He imagined his lovely young Kirsty running along the path to welcome him home. 'My child,' he called.

Kirsty's voice came through a little more urgently. 'Father, listen to me.'

Colin nodded, still in his dream. 'I see you, Kirsty.'

'Ye canna,' the voice said, 'I'm out here.'

'Aye.' Suddenly Colin came to and snapped up. 'Och, I must be dreaming.' He looked around him wildly. 'Kirsty!' he called.

Kirsty's voice came through the porthole.

'Whist, Father,' she said, 'keep your voice down.'

'Where are ye?' Colin said.

'In a boat,' said Kirsty, 'outside here.'

Colin turned, looked out of the porthole, and put his hand through to clasp Kirsty's soft one. 'My Kirsty.' Colin was in tears. 'Are you well, child? You've come to no harm?'

Kirsty nodded, also unable to keep the tears from her eyes. 'I'm aye fine. And ye, Father?'

'Much better,' Colin whispered, 'a world better for hearing your voice, child. But you canna stay here. They'll find ye.'

'Then quickly, Father,' said Kirsty, 'take this.'

She passed him a pistol through the porthole and Colin pulled it in, amazed. 'It's a miracle. I must be in a dream.'

'Nae dream, Father,' Kirsty's voice came through, 'we have arms for all of you, and a plan. Now come closer.' Colin put his ear to the porthole. 'Listen to me.'

15

The Fight for the Brig

Grey glanced meaningfully over at Perkins, then looked back to the Doctor. 'You drive a hard bargain Doctor, but no matter. We agree. Now where is the Prince?'

'The very last place you'd think to look for him,' said the Doctor.

'Well?'

'Right here on this ship.' The listening men broke away in disbelief.

Trask reached for his sword hilt again. 'Let me have him,' he said.

Grey's thin mouth curled. 'A dangerous jest, Doctor.'

The Doctor nodded eagerly. 'Did you mark the young Highlander with me? The piper?'

'Piper?' Grey tried to remember, then shook his head.

'With soft hands and face. Did you notice his hair?' He looked around. First Trask, then Grey, then Perkins all shook their heads. 'Unmistakable,' the Doctor went on. 'He is the Prince.'

Despite themselves, the others were now carried along by the Doctor's earnest manner, which was in such contrast to his former flippancy.

Grey leaned forward once more, his eyes searching the Doctor's face. 'You had better be very sure.'

'Would I have come here and placed my life in your hands if I had not been very sure?' said the Doctor, his green eyes wide open, projecting the child-like candour he could turn on when he wanted to.

Trask, anyway, was convinced. He slammed his hand on the table, then swung towards the door. 'We'll smell out the Pretender right now, by heaven.'

Grey nodded. 'Perkins,' he said. But Perkins needed no further bidding. He followed Trask to the door.

'One moment,' said the Doctor, 'aren't you forgetting something?'

Grey turned back. 'What?'

'I'm the only one here who knows what he looks like.'

'He's right,' said Perkins. The others looked back suspiciously for a moment and then Grey nodded his head.

'Then come you with us. Hurry!'

With Trask's hand on his arm, the Doctor was pulled out of the cabin.

Down below in the hold, all was apparently as before. Colin, Jamie and Willy seemed as deeply asleep as the other men, all wrapped in their long tartan plaids. The door at the top of the companionway creaked open and Trask appeared holding a lantern. He started climbing down quietly, followed by Grey, Perkins, the Doctor and two armed sailors.

As they assembled at the bottom of the ladder, Grey held his hand to his lips. 'Proceed softly,' he said. 'If they suspect whom we're searching for and know to be here, we'll have a riot on our hands.'

Holding the lantern high, they started to move forward across the crowded deck, examining the faces of the sleeping men as they went. As Trask held his lantern above the Highlanders, the Doctor examined each one in turn, shaking his head and leading them further and further towards the far end of the hold.

'Well, Doctor?' came Grey's impatient whisper. 'Is there no sign of him?'

'Perhaps he's further over,' said the Doctor. He pointed to the far side of the room where Colin and Jamie could be made out by the porthole. 'That looks like him over there.'

Not liking his tone, Grey's voice dropped into a silky menace. 'If you've made a mistake, Doctor.'

'No,' said the Doctor, 'that is him, there!' He pointed over to Jamie, his voice raised, just as the entire floor came to life.

'Creag an tuire.' Jamie's high pitched voice rang over the room as the Highlanders leapt to their feet – swords, pistols and muskets at the ready.

'No firearms, lads,' Colin called, but his advice was unnecessary. As the two sailors turned to run for the companionway, they found a dozen swords at their throats. Grey, Perkins and Trask were similarly surrounded. Only Trask, pulling his large cutlass, made a fight for it at the far end, cutting down the Highlander opposite him. Swinging the huge cutlass back and forth, he cleared a path for himself until his back was against the wall.

'You'll not get Henry Trask alive,' he called.

The Highlanders drew back until Willy came forward, holding his lantern. 'I dinna want ye alive, Trask,' said Willy.

Trask's face fell for a moment as he saw his old adversary. Then he leaped forward, raising the cutlass and swinging it in a blow that had it landed would have taken Willy's head from his shoulders. But Willy, stepping back, handed the lantern to Jamie and brought his own sword up.

'Keep back, lads, he's mine,' called Willy.

The Highlanders watched as the two men, their swords flashing as they sought an opening in the narrow deck space, fell to in furious combat.

Meanwhile, Jamie ran to the companionway and, sword in one hand, lantern in the other, turned to the others. 'Follow me, lads,' he said. 'The fight's not over yet.' He clambered up and out onto the deck, followed by the Highlanders.

Willy, weakened by his long confinement, was getting the worst of the fight. He appeared to falter, and his cutlass dropped.

Trask lunged forward eagerly. 'I have you now,' he said. But Willy, with a flick of the wrist, knocked Task's cutlass up and stabbed home in Trask's shoulder.

'I'm relieving you of your command, Captain Trask,' he said.

But the large, fearsome Trask was not yet done for. His cutlass slashed Willy's arm. 'Not yet,' he said. As Willy fell back wounded, Trask ran for the companionway and the deck.

Up on deck, Jamie and the Highlanders were fighting the sailors of the *Annabelle*. They had now cornered them on the poop. Two sailors lay dead, and one Highlander was nursing his wounds on the sky-light, when Trask appeared.

'To me, boys,' he called. 'I'm still master here.'

Ben appeared from behind the mast. 'Not for long, mate,' he said.

Trask reacted for a moment at the apparition of someone he considered dead. 'You?' he said. 'I'll make sure of thee this time, boy.'

He raised his cutlass just as Jamie swung over the poop on the end of a rope and with all his force kicked Trask over the side of the *Annabelle* into the dark waiting waters.

'Ah,' said Ben, a little disappointed. 'I was gonna try my karate on him.'

'What?' said Jamie.

'Karate,' said Ben.

'Och,' Jamie turned away. 'Whatever that is, it would not have worked against that monster.'

The wounded Willy MacKay had now appeared on deck, his arm bound. 'Where's Trask?' he called.

Jamie pointed over the side. 'In the firth.'

Willy nodded. 'Good man.' He called out to the men

still struggling on the deck. 'Hold hard! Stop fighting, all of ye.'

The Highlanders drew back. The sailors reluctantly lowered their swords. 'Listen men,' he said. Willy hauled himself up the ladder to the poop. 'I need sailors. We're sailing to France by the morning tide. Who'll volunteer?'

There was a moment's hesitation on the part of the sailors then, realizing that they had little option, one man after another stepped forward.

Willy nodded, satisfied. 'Good lads,' he said. 'Mind ye, if ye hadna volunteered you'd've had a long cold swim for it. Right,' he said, 'away wi'ye. Make ready, we sail in an hour.'

The Doctor now appeared: walking over to the rail, he looked down and signalled, then helped Polly and Kirsty up on the deck.

Kirsty ran over to Colin, who was leaning, still a little weak from his wound, against the mast. While Kirsty hugged her father, Polly, much to Ben's embarrassment, flung her arms around the Doctor and Ben.

''Ere,' said Ben, 'leave off, Pol.'

'I won't,' said Polly, kissing him on the cheek. 'We won, we won.'

'For the moment,' said the Doctor.

'What do you mean, Doctor?' said Polly. None of them noticed Jamie standing beside them listening intensely.

'Don't you see, Pol,' said Ben, 'the real job's just starting. We've got to get back to the TARDIS with only a rough idea where it is, and the whole British army out looking for us.'

'What are we going to do then?' said Polly, a little dashed.

'Get ashore before they cast anchor, right Doctor?'

The Doctor nodded, then went over to Willy and Colin. If the others had been looking, they would have seen Jamie turn and disappear over the side of the brig.

Willy, once more the master on his own deck, was preparing the *Annabelle* for her voyage. 'Stand by the capstan,' he called. He pointed to a knot of Highlanders who were watching uncertainly. 'You men help them.' Aided by the Highland prisoners, the crew started raising the anchor slowly.

The Doctor tapped Willy on the shoulder. 'We must return ashore now,' he said.

'Do what you will, man,' said Willy impatiently. He turned. 'Stand by the halyards,' he called, then looked up to where the remaining crew were unfurling the large square sails of the brig.

The Doctor went over to where Colin and Kirsty were standing. Beside them, held at swordpoint, Perkins and Grey were sitting on the skylight. The little clerk was looking around anxiously, but Grey, as aloof as ever, seemed unperturbed by the complete change in his fortunes.

The Doctor turned as Colin came over to them. 'What will we do with the prisoners here?' – indicating Perkins and the solicitor.

The Doctor looked. 'I think we'll take Solicitor Grey along with us, as a hostage.'

'And Perkins?' said Colin.

Perkins, hearing his name, jumped up. 'Oh, Laird,' he said to Colin, 'may I have converse with you?'

'Ye are,' said Colin.

'I beg of you,' said Perkins, 'do not send me ashore with that man.' He pointed to Grey. 'If you go to France, you'll need a secretary. Especially' – he drew himself up to his full five foot four inches – 'one familiar with the French tongue.'

Colin laughed at the self-important little man. 'Shifting with the wind now, are ye, ye rogue.' He turned. 'Well Doctor, what do you think?'

'Can any of your people speak French?' said the Doctor.

Colin shook his head. 'But little, I'm afraid,' he said. 'Then use him,' said the Doctor, 'I've no doubt he'll be loyal enough.'

Perkins, immensely relieved, started rubbing his hands. 'Oh sir, I will, I will.'

'Until the wind shifts again,' said the Doctor.

He turned back to Colin. 'We must go.' He looked over at the Highlanders guarding Grey. 'Set him over the side in that boat.'

Grey glared at Perkins, and stood up. The little man turned, raised his stubby fingers, and snapped them in the solicitor's face. 'Mr Grey, sir, I have always wanted to do that. You've no idea the pleasure that gave me.' But the cold glare of Grey's eyes made him back away, as the solicitor was led to the rail and helped over the side into the waiting boat.

With Ben at the oars, the boat sped across the waters to the waiting wharf. As they reached it, they looked back at the dark shape of the brig.

'I can't even see the ship now,' said Polly.

'They're going to signal to us just before they go.' He looked. 'There it is.'

A small pinpoint of light waved briefly across the estuary and then vanished.

'I wish Jamie had said goodbye to us,' said Polly. 'I looked for him, but he disappeared. This is what Kirsty gave me as a parting present.' She held up a small silver thistle brooch. 'I'm really going to miss them,' she said. 'Do you think they'll beat the English blockade?'

The Doctor nodded. 'The fog will help them.' Then he shook his head ruefully. 'More than it'll help us. We've a long, hard journey back to the TARDIS across the Highlands. I don't know how we're ever going to find our way.'

As he spoke, a plaid bundle in the bow of the boat was flung back, and Jamie's face appeared. 'I'll guide you,' he said.

'Jamie!' Polly called, delighted.

'Why didn't you go with the others?' said Ben.

'Let's say I fancy mah chances here better.'

'How did you know where we were going,' said Ben, suspiciously.

'I listened to ye,' said Jamie.

The Doctor nodded and smiled. 'We're very glad to have you with us, Jamie.'

'Won't you be in danger here, though?' said Polly.

'Och, if you can survive here, then so can I.'

They clambered ashore heaving the solicitor, his arms now effectively bound with cord by Ben, across the jetty.

'Now, back to the barn . . .' began the Doctor, then froze as the unmistakable sound of marching men came to them.

'It's an English patrol,' said Ben. 'Quick.' He looked around. 'In here.' Pulling Grey with them, they opened the door of a boathouse at the end of the jetty and hurried inside. The boathouse was dark and smelled strongly of fish. They could just make out the dark shapes of a row of upturned boats as they crouched down, hardly daring to breathe as the marching feet came nearer.

Polly peered through a small crack in the door. Outside she could make out a squad of red-coated soldiers, led by a sergeant with a lantern.

'Right,' the sergeant turned to his men. 'You two,' he pointed to the soldiers in the leading rank, 'you stay here and keep a watch for escaping rebels. They may try to get across to the boats out in the firth.' The sergeant turned and looked down along the empty jetty. 'Strange,' he said, 'I could have sworn there was a sentry mounted here when I came by earlier.' He turned back. 'Right about turn, quick march.' The soldiers marched off.

Ben straightened up. 'Have they gone?' he said.

Polly turned. 'No,' she whispered, 'they've left two men here.'

At that moment, Grey, seeing his chance, called out, 'Help me!' he cried. 'Help!'

Ben, who had shifted his hand off the solicitor's mouth, now clamped it back on again. But the damage was done. The two sentinels who had been making themselves comfortable on one of the pair of bollards rose to their feet and looked suspiciously over at the boathouse.

'They've heard us,' said Polly. 'They're coming this way.'

The two soldiers moved cautiously over towards the boathouse. One turned to the other. 'What d'you think, Bill,' he said.

'Dunno,' said his mate, 'could have been a cat, I suppose.'

'Well, we'd better find out,' said the other one, and they opened the door of the boathouse.

The soldiers entered, muskets and bayonets at the ready, and looked around. All they could see was the long row of upturned boats, like huge black beetles.

'Nothing here, Bill.' They turned to go just as Grey, twisting out of Ben's grasp, called, 'Rebels, watch yourselves.'

The soldiers turned around just as Ben and Jamie, who'd been waiting in the dark, each flung themselves on to a soldier. Taken unawares in their cumbersome uniforms, the soldiers were no match for Ben and Jamie, and both were quickly overpowered – Jamie with his dirk held at his man's throat, Ben with his soldier face down on the ground and the man's hand held up behind him in a strong half-nelson grip.

Suddenly Polly screamed. 'The window,' she called.

They turned to look, but it was too late, their captive had gone. Ben dashed towards the door, picking up one of the soldier's muskets, but the Doctor stopped him.

'No Ben, you'll bring all the guards down upon us. Let him go.'

Ben turned to the Doctor. 'But he was our hostage, wasn't he? We could have used him to get us safely back to the TARDIS.'

The Doctor nodded. 'Yes,' he said, then he smiled. 'We'll just have to find someone else.' He turned to Polly. 'Won't we, Polly?'

Polly looked blank and then, catching on, smiled back at the Doctor.

16

Algernon Again

Algernon Ffinch was sitting outside the officers' quarters
of the main British army barracks in Inverness. Leaning
back against the doorpost, his face flushed with wine, he
was half asleep, but trying to keep awake. He had
returned seeking his bed, only to run into the
Honourable Colonel Attwood, his commander, who was
getting together a four for whist. The Colonel's request
was the same as a command. When Colonel Attwood
wanted to play whist, you sat down and played with him,
and took your losses like a man. Otherwise, the next time
a chance of promotion came your way, you were apt to
be forgotten in favour of some more accommodating
officer. Now, just as he was dropping off, he suddenly
felt something hard and cold touch his temple. His eyes
opened, he turned to see Ben standing there with a
pistol, half-concealed with his coat, at the Lieutenant's
head.

'What the –' he began.

'We want your company, mate,' said Ben.

A familiar voice came from behind Algernon. 'I know
you won't refuse me, Algy.'

'Oh no.' Algernon turned. There was Polly, smiling
sweetly, her hand on his shoulder. 'Oh, this is r-r-really
too much,' he said.

'Quickly,' said Polly, 'this way.'

The Doctor, standing beside Polly, reached out his
hand and helped Algernon, still half stupefied with wine,

to his feet and started to lead him away just as a tall, red-faced man with grey hair and a fierce military moustache appeared at the door: the redoubtable, Honourable Colonel Attwood. He also was flushed with drink, and held a pack of cards in his hand. 'Damne man, where the devil do you think you're going?'

Algernon, despite his fuddled state, snapped to attention. 'Colonel,' he said.

'Have you forgotten man, it's your deal, Ffinch,' he said indignantly. He held up the pack of cards.

'Y-yes,' said Algernon. 'B-but . . .'

The Colonel raised the lorgnette dangling from his lapel and inspected Polly, Ben, and the Doctor. 'And who are these vagabonds?'

The Doctor bowed very low, putting on his German accent. 'Doctor von Verner, at your service, Colonel. Remedies for the ague, warts, the twitch, the colic, and . . .' he glanced down at the Colonel's slippered feet, 'for the gout, sir.'

The Colonel leaned back, a little overwhelmed by all this. 'Gout, man? I haven't got gout.'

The Doctor rushed on quickly. 'But that's not why I'm here, sir. Oh no, I wouldn't waste your time with that. A fine healthy gentleman like yourself. It's just, this ring, you see, sir . . .' He held up the Prince's ring.

Algernon, his fuddled thoughts clearing, now saw an opportunity to get away from the Doctor without compromising himself. 'Uh, perhaps,' he coughed, 'we'd better get back to the game, sir. The night air, you know, and all that.'

'Blast the night air,' said the Colonel. 'Let me see that.' He snatched the ring from the Doctor. 'By gad,' he said, 'the Pretender's shield. Where did you get this from?'

The Doctor stood back and waved his hand. 'Vell, sir,' he said, 'you go up there and over there, and then round to your left, and then a little to the right, and then, vell, we were taking the Lieutenant there, you see.'

Algernon put his hand to his head. 'Uh, the game, sir,' he said.

'Confound the game,' said the Colonel, 'this is the Prince's ring. Now go with them, Ffinch, there's a good fellow. Take a detachment.'

'Ach, nein, sir, nein,' said the Doctor, putting his finger to his nose.

Colonel Attwood was not used to being contradicted. 'What man?'

The Doctor went on quickly. 'It would alarm the rascals, sir. We are enough to capture him. If we take some soldiers, he will see us coming.'

'Hmmm,' the Colonel considered for moment. 'You're right.' He turned around. 'What are you waiting for, Lieutenant, you have your orders.'

Algernon saluted weakly. 'But sir, this wench here,' he pointed to Polly, and as he did so, Polly, who was wearing Algernon's identification disc around her neck, started pulling it out. 'No, sir,' Algernon went on. 'No, sir, very good sir, very . . .' Again Algernon saluted, turned, and started moving off with Ben and Polly on each side.

The Doctor paused for a moment. The Colonel turned to him. 'Oh, when you have him . . .' he said.

The Doctor nodded and winked. 'Ve must bring him straight to you. Right, sir?'

The Colonel smiled and nodded. 'Good chap,' he said. 'Good chap.'

The Doctor touched his hat and scurried off to the others.

'Oh,' the Colonel had one final thought. He called after the Doctor. 'You don't play whist by any chance, do you?'

The Doctor turned back. 'Ach, unfortunately no, sir. Vhy?'

'Oh, nothing, never mind. Later, perhaps.' And the Colonel turned around and went back into the barracks.

17

A Return to the Cottage

Several hours later, having retraced the weary miles from Inverness to Culloden Moor, the Doctor and his friends, still with Lieutenant Ffinch in tow, arrived back at the cottage. Polly, who felt that Algernon was her special charge, had tried to make the Lieutenant's load lighter by keeping up a ceaseless flow of chatter, only a quarter of which Ffinch had comprehended. But Ben and the Doctor noticed that while he resented taking orders from them, Polly could, as Ben put it, twist him around her little finger.

They arrived back at the cottage just as the early sun was warming the air on the moor. As they stood outside, Jamie and Ben looked up at the ropes still hanging from the tree.

'I won't forget this place in a hurry,' said Ben.

The Doctor turned to Algernon Ffinch. 'I don't know how we can ever thank you, Lieutenant. We could never have made it without your help.' Indeed, there had been four brushes with English patrols, at each of which the Lieutenant had concocted a story that enabled them to go on their way.

'I told him all about Mr Grey's activities,' said Polly.

Ben nodded. 'Yeah, you better nab him quick. He's slippery, that geezer.'

'In that case,' said Algernon, 'I had better start looking for the detachment I left down here under Sergeant Klegg. Leave the British soldier too long to his own devices, and lord knows what can happen.'

Polly came forward, took the Lieutenant's identification disc from around her neck, and then rather tenderly brought out the lock of his hair from her pouch. 'Here,' she said, 'you deserve these back now.'

'Ah, yes,' said Ffinch. He took the identification disc from her a little embarrassed, then handed her back the lock of hair. 'If you'd like . . .' he began.

Polly nodded, her eyes bright. 'I'd love to,' she said. She took the lock of hair and tenderly placed it back in her pouch, just as a line of red-coated soldiers appeared from around the side of the cottage with Grey at their head.

Jamie and Ben reached for the pistols stuck in their belts, but the Doctor stopped them quickly. Resistance was useless. The troops who had been concealed around the cottage, now came out of hiding, some twenty of them with levelled muskets. The Doctor put his hands up in the air, followed by Ben and Jamie.

'I thought you would return here, Doctor,' Grey's voice was precise and silken with menace.

He bowed to Algernon with just a touch of irony in his manner and voice. 'May I congratulate you on having caught these rebels, Lieutenant. I'm sure it will lead to promotion for you.'

The Sergeant in charge of the detachment came over and saluted. 'Lieutenant Ffinch, sir.'

Algernon looked at him. 'Ah, Sergeant Klegg, I'm glad to see you.' He looked around. 'And my men,' he said. 'Good work, Sergeant.'

Grey had been standing somewhat impatiently while the Lieutenant and the Sergeant exchanged courtesies. Now he came forward, speaking curtly to the Lieutenant. 'You can escort them back to Inverness with me, Lieutenant. We'll see that this rogue,' he pointed to the Doctor, 'and his confederates do not escape the gallows this time.'

Polly turned to him. 'We spared your life, Mr Grey,' she said. 'Don't you think you owe us one for that?'

Grey stepped past Ffinch and the sergeant and looked at her. 'Certainly, my fine lady,' he said. 'I'll spare you the gallows. Instead, I'll have you whipped at the tail of a cart from one end of Inverness to the other.' His eyes glowed. 'I'll have you whipped until—'

'Enough!' Grey turned in surprise. Algernon Ffinch stepped forward, furious.

Grey looked back at him, coldly. 'Were you talking to me, sir?'

'Yes, sir,' said Algernon, 'I've heard the whole story of your schemes from this young lady here.'

'What?' Grey stepped back.

The Doctor stepped forward. 'Wicked times we live in. A prison commissioner using his office to smuggle rebels out of the country.'

Grey turned back, his eyes more snakelike than ever, almost hissing as he spoke. 'You're wasting your breath, Doctor, it was all perfectly legal. The prisoners chose to sign the contracts of transportation to the Colonies.'

'Contracts?' said the Doctor. 'I don't believe I saw any contracts. Did you, Ben?'

'Wouldn't know what they was,' said Ben. 'Would you?' he turned to Jamie.

'I ken nothing about contracts,' said Jamie.

For the first time, Grey appeared a little flustered. 'A lie, Lieutenant,' he said. 'The contracts were signed, and I have them right here.' He felt in his pocket . . . then his face changed colour. He patted the other pocket, then the other. 'I know they were—'

The Doctor shook his head. 'Tut, tut,' he said. 'Sad, isn't it? Once a promising legal talent, too.'

Grey turned desperately, seeing the game was up. 'I warn you, Lieutenant, if you—'

'I've had enough of your warnings, and your threats.' Ffinch turned to the Sergeant. 'Gag him, and take him to prison under escort.'

The Sergeant saluted, then hesitated. 'Uhm . . . and these prisoners, sir?' he said.

'I'll take care of them,' said Algernon. 'After all,' he said, 'they are Crown witnesses against that rogue.' He pointed to the fuming Grey. 'I'll rejoin you later, Sergeant.'

The Sergeant saluted, turned around, called his men to order and, with Grey marching between them, the Redcoats set out down the track away from the cottage. No one spoke until the last Redcoat had turned the corner. Then Polly, wide-eyed, turned back to Algernon.

'Algy,' she said, 'why did you do all this?'

Algernon stiffened, his eyes looking above her head. 'A chance to put paid to a villain, ma'am.'

Polly went up to him and put her hand on his tunic. 'It wasn't just that – was it?'

Algernon cleared his throat. 'Uh . . . not quite, ma'am.'

'Polly,' said Polly softly.

'Polly,' said Algernon. 'I must go.'

'Thank you, Algernon Alfred,' To the Lieutenant's intense embarrassment, Polly put her arms around his neck and kissed him goodbye. As she did so, a string of musket shots burst from the moor.

The Lieutenant, his face scarlet, turned to the Doctor. 'I wouldn't linger here, you know, they're still scouring the moors for rebels.' He saluted, gave one last look at Polly, and then marched quickly after his men.

'Whoopee!' Ben yelled. 'Now let's get back to the TARDIS.'

'Do you know where it is?' said Polly.

Ben nodded. 'You bet, just over the hill there.'

'TARDIS?' Jamie looked at them.

Polly smiled. 'You'll understand in time.'

'Aye,' Jamie shook his head, 'there's much I do not understand. Where did those contracts vanish to?'

'Yes, Doc,' said Ben. 'Where did they go?'

The Doctor backed away from them. 'I haven't the foggiest idea,' he said, 'unless . . .' he felt in his pockets.

Ben and Polly looked at each other. They knew exactly what was coming.

'You old fraud,' said Ben.

'Well,' said the Doctor, 'imagine that.' He extracted three large parchment sheets from his pocket and proceeded to tear them into shreds.

'Come on, Doc,' said Ben. 'We must go.'

'What about Jamie?' said Polly. 'We can't leave him here.'

'Ah, true,' said the Doctor, 'the ship has gone. And he won't get far on these moors.'

Polly turned to Jamie. 'What will you do, Jamie?' she said.

'Och,' said Jamie, 'I'll be all right. They nae will catch me.'

There was another ragged chorus of muskets, a little nearer this time.

'Hear that?' said Ben. 'If we don't move fast, they'll catch us all.'

Polly turned to the Doctor. 'Can Jamie come with us, Doctor?'

The Doctor looked doubtful for a minute, and then his face cleared. 'Well, if you promise to teach me all you know about the bagpipes . . .'

Jamie nodded. 'If that's what ye want, Doctor.'

Ben groaned, putting his hand to his ears. 'That's all we need aboard the TARDIS,' he said.

Polly took Jamie's arm. 'Come on, Jamie boy.'

They hurried off, following the track that they had taken down the hill, which now seemed a long, long time ago.

As they came into the hollow where they had left the time-machine, it seemed for a moment as if the TARDIS had disappeared. Then, through the clustering brambles, they made out the familiar blue shape of the police box. Ben pulled away some brambles, the Doctor waved his hand, and the door slid open.

'It seems all right,' said the Doctor, a little fussily. 'I'd better check the engines.' He went inside, followed by Ben.

Jamie, suddenly afraid of the strange looking object, hung back. He was going with these strange people into something he only dimly comprehended. Where would they take him? Would he ever see his native glen again?

As he hesitated, Polly turned back and grasped his hand. 'Don't be afraid,' she said, 'it's much nicer inside than it is out. There's so many wonderful surprises waiting for you, you'll see.'

Jamie allowed himself to be drawn through into the small police box. The door closed behind him and he saw to his astonishment the large, hexagonal, brightly-lighted interior of the time-machine.